HUMANVILLE

CYNTHIA FRENCH

D1707560

HARRY MAX PUBLISHING CO. INC.
NASHVILLE, TN.

*This book is dedicated to my father
and mother, Gilbert and Carolyn French.
Thank you for believing in me. I love you.*

FOREWORD

The last thing I ever thought I'd do is write a book. *That* particular goal was nowhere in my dreams. Singing was my only focus. After many years in the music industry, I found myself continually feeling unfulfilled, even after achieving some success. The main reason for this sense of frustration was the fact that I dealt with anorexia and bulimia for most of my teenage years and adulthood. This was a big part of my life, and the diseases prevented me from fulfilling my potential. They also kept me in a virtual prison for many, many years.

Through a miracle, I overcame eating disorders and desired to somehow share my story with others who have lived (or are living) in the nightmare I'd been in. I wanted to avoid writing the typical "woe is me" self-help book that might run the risk of being too self-indulgent, so I decided to create a story that would incorporate my experiences, but could be read as a fable.

Last fall, a man I'd recently started dating asked me to accompany him on a trip to Hawaii. I said yes, and suddenly was swept away on a "pretend honeymoon." After about four days of secluded "bliss," this budding romance failed to blossom. What did bloom, though, was something much more phenomenal. The idea for this book was born.

I had an esoteric concept about how to approach this challenge, but while in Hawaii, a conversation with my date planted a seed in my imagination.

Upon returning from my trip, I sat down at my computer and began typing. Eleven months and at least forty edits later, *Humanville* became a finished novel.

For those of you who read this book, my sincere desire is that you will find strength in the knowledge that God does, indeed, live in all of us and that we are worthy of self-love because we are a part of God, and God is a part of us. An old message, a new messenger.

Creating and writing this story has been the most rewarding (yet challenging) experience I've ever had. I'm honored you have chosen to read *Humanville*, and pray that it will give you encouragement, enjoyment, and most importantly, hope.

HUMANVILLE

Hello, My Friend,

I'm so sorry it's taken awhile to sit down and write to you. I planned on explaining as soon as I figured everything out, but time flies, and I got caught up with...well, more than I ever thought could be possible, really. I want to make it up to you, so if you don't mind, let me start from the beginning and fill in the details so you won't think I've been a total space cadet. There's so much to tell you!

It all started when I got home from a rather intense evening. I'd been out with my friends on a typical "girls night." These usually started with all of us meeting at one of our favorite restaurants for drinks and dinner. Then we'd change venues and pursue dancing, drinking, flirting, and whatever else came our way. Most of us were single (although two were married, but not happily). We'd commiserate over how lonely, frustrated, or angry we were about something. Misery was what we all had in common. Fortunately, we'd drink and eat our problems away during the evening, and briefly have what we considered a good time. The quick fix.

This particular evening had been a kicker because one of us (no, not me!) had been angry with her boyfriend of two years. They'd argued over the "when are we going to get married" issue because he was dragging his feet. She got totally smashed (and god knows what else—some bathroom action, if you know what I mean), and proceeded to get so wild that she did a strip tease on the dance floor. She then crawled on top of the piano, belted out a painfully bad song that was obviously being created as she went along, then made out with every man she could get her hands on and any woman who was too drunk to notice. The night ended with my friend getting into a cat fight with a waitress and giving her a black eye. The police were called, she flipped them off and was immediately hauled away to the police station. We had to follow her downtown (being very careful to not draw attention to our own intoxicated condition), call her boyfriend (who was furious), and then sit there for two hours before he showed up. During this time we watched a stream of people parade through the police station...prostitutes, victims of robberies, petty crime violators, and a homeless guy arrested for loitering. There was one major commotion involving a drug bust that brought in five pushers and a slew of officers surrounding them. Finally, Mr. Boyfriend showed up and we called it an evening.

I got home about 3:30 a.m. and couldn't sleep, so I turned on the television. The all night news station was reporting a story about a man who had murdered his wife to collect insurance money. Supposedly, he was having an affair and wanted to start a new life with his sweetie and needed a little nest egg, and no wife to worry about. The next story was about a teenage girl who had abandoned her two-day old infant in a trash bin. The baby had died and she was being charged with murder. Then came the report about the guy who was scamming elderly couples by selling them non-existent time-shares. He had spent all the money, leaving most of the couples penniless and facing financial ruin. The news went on and on with similar stories for the next thirty minutes.

As I started to drift off to sleep, something dawned on me that caused my mind to pause for a second. I'd just watched one of my best friends go out of her mind and get arrested, spent hours in a police station observing *that* crazy scene, and listened to a newsperson report on terrible crimes. None of it had fazed me. I hadn't even given it a second thought, for the most part. It was all just a part of daily life, a typical day in the city. I shook my head, rolled over, and closed my eyes. This was where I lived, and people here were accustomed to looking the other way. Why should I be different? For some reason, though, sleep escaped me. I couldn't stop thinking about the "cat fight," the police station, and the news reports. I was bothered. What was causing me to think about all of these things now? Something deep inside, subconscious, was making me feel unsettled, but I couldn't define it. Finally, I got up and took a sleeping pill and that took care of everything, at least temporarily. The quick fix...

You see, I lived in Humanville—considered the most incredible city in the world. I was one of its most impressive citizens. The quick fix is what it was all about here. I, like most of the people I knew, didn't want to waste time and energy on anything that didn't directly pertain to my own life. Oh, yeah, I'd follow my drunken friend down to the police station, but only because of obligation, not because I wanted to. She got herself into that mess. I was just, well, playing a role...yeah, that's right. It's what we do in Humanville.

If this sounds familiar to you, there's a reason for that. Not that you were there, of course, but in some ways, I'm sure you can relate to the scenario. I mean, who hasn't been in a scene like that at least once? You know, a little bizarre, but at the same time, it doesn't even compute as real because you're so programmed to not pay attention? Well, little did I know that this particular night was going to lead to something I'd never been through before. I was really good at being programmed to not feel, so the events I'm about to share with you completely knocked me for a loop!

~

When I discovered it was time to tell you my story, I have to admit that nerves overtook me for a minute. I suddenly realized I was about to "go public" and freaked out a little. I immediately thought "Aww, man! Do I have to re-hash everything? Why can't I just *not* do it and tell everyone I *thought* about doing it?" I figured that might take care of any responsibility I felt about being open with my past life...but...no, no, no can do. Gotta tell you, gotta be honest. I mean, I really have no choice, and the truth is, I'm excited about sharing my tale with you. It's part of my purpose, so that makes it very cool. It's just that, every once in a while I still go through a moment of "Humanville" thinking, as I call it. Once I get in there, though, I think a rhythm will kick in and I'll get the knack of storytelling. I do know that the key to successful writing is to "reel you in at the beginning". In other words, I need to be extremely interesting and charming enough to keep you here with me. Hmm...ok, I'll try this...

Have you ever thought about what your purpose really is, or why you were here? Do you ever question whether you are really doing in life what you think you are meant to do? How about wondering if you're utilizing your talents and gifts to the best of your ability? Ok, fess up, do you feel fulfilled?

Oops, sorry... that's not it...now I sound like one of those self-help courses that try to get you to acknowledge how screwed up you are. No worries, I'm not about to do *that* to you. I just have to get my "creative gloves" on tighter and try again...this set-up business is challenging...hmm....if there was ever a time to regret not taking a creative writing course in school, this is it. I'm procrastinating...it's pretty obvious. I'm amused with myself and am already fighting the urge to take a break because I usually can't sit still long enough to even get through a movie!

Now...focus...patience...focus...patience...hmm... I wonder if I can type standing up? Ok, I'm drifting ...all right, here we go...

~

I'm going to get into this thing by showing you a part of my personality I'm not very proud of. It's not pretty, I warn you, but for you to fully grasp everything I'm going to tell you, it's got to be done. Now remember, I'm sooo much cooler now, but as a responsible writer, I've got to cover all angles of the story. (Just pretend you buy that line of you know what, ok? Thanks.)

Ooohhh, I don't want to do this…all right, I might as well get it over with… This used to be me…

ME

My name is Desmond Durango. No, I didn't make it up. Believe it or not, that's my real name. Amazing, isn't it? As you've probably noticed, everything about me is amazing, really. I have no doubt that you find me very intriguing, because most people do. I receive a lot of attention, and I live for that. I'll tell you a little about myself, since I'm sure you were going to ask ...

I live in a very trendy part of the city and am considered a mover and shaker. I've had much success as a singer—singing back up on a number of big albums, and have toured in the same capacity with two of the most successful bands in music. I also model—my agency is one of the most prestigious in Humanville. I'm a high profile person, being recognized most places I go(which is very important)and because of powerful friends and acquaintances, I'm invited to the best parties. This is a big deal, being on the right guest lists. I'm also able to get into any club I go to and can finagle a good table at most restaurants. With the help of my long and thick auburn hair, piercing green eyes, smooth skin, and gazelle-like stature, I turn quite a few heads when I enter a room. You see, this is what it is all about for me—image.

I live in the right area, drive the right car, wear the right designers, and say the right things. I am perfect...at least I work hard to make people think I am. My career at times has been phenomenal, which is the biggest high...I get so much attention. But, on occasion has faltered...which, of course I don't talk about! I've done my best, though, to make sure that even in the down times, socially I'm still "in the loop." This in itself has been a full-time job, but it's important to be accepted by the "right" people. Life depends on it, in my opinion.

I do pretty well in this arena, I must say. Although I'm always under extreme stress and strain, I have persevered and held on to my position in Humanville society. It's required extraordinary energy, but I mean, what else matters than being accepted by the people who are "important"!?!

Success means everything to me, and I define success as money and power. Nothing short of that will do. Well, fame is important, too...can't leave that one out. I keep my priorities straight by not wasting time on anyone or anything that won't advance my career and goals.

I've dated a number of famous and powerful men and if I told you who some of them were, you wouldn't believe it. I don't plan on being tied down to one person right now. Too confining. I need my freedom. I have to network and socialize with the people who can give me what I want in life. If I let a man get too close or become needy, I will become trapped...I won't have that! There is always someone "bigger and better" out there to help me if I'm free to find him. I've got to play the game better than anyone else to get what I want. My mantra is, "Stay one step ahead of the competi- tion...always" and that's what I plan on doing. I have to win, no matter what it takes!!!

~

Whoa, that was painful! That used to be me...well, the frightened part of me. Pretty disgusting, isn't it? There *was* a time I was that self-absorbed and misguided. Of course, I wasn't so blatant about it, but inside felt the need to emit the image in order to be accepted. In truth, it was all a cover-up to hide my insecurity and lack of confidence. I was deeply afraid of life, and wore a defensive coat of arms to protect me from others just like me. However, "birds of a feather flock together," and fear was what bonded my community of Humanville together.

I didn't consciously know my existence was encased in such a plastic shell. I was so obsessed with looking like "the package " that I didn't *feel* anything, and wasn't a real person. I missed out on so much life!

Looking back, it makes sense that I'd find myself in a world that was based so much on image and perfection, for I was raised to live in it. My personal history is founded on the guidelines of Humanville, and I carried everything I learned into adulthood...

THE BEGINNING

I started life with two intact parents and an older sister. More siblings came later. From the outside, it looked like a pretty normal upbringing, but I personally never felt "normal." Maybe part of it was that my name was Desmond, which apparently is a boy's name. I'd *like* to tell you my parents were very chic hippies who thought it was cool to use a boy's name for a girl, but the truth is they weren't. They were just hoping for a boy. When I came out, my mom was too drugged and my dad, in his shaken state, blurted out my name to the doctor without really considering I was a girl. This was the name they'd agreed upon for their son. You'd think they'd have thought of one for a girl, too, but I guess they just didn't get that far in the planning stuff to come up with one. So, Desmond ended up on the birth certificate, and Desmond was what I was stuck with. For the most part, the only detrimental issue I've suffered from my dad's blunder is having to explain the name a lot. Also, I had to send back all the army and marine recruiting literature I received as a teenager…you know the ones that say they are looking for "a few good men." I'd just write them back and say, "Yeah, me too!!"

My parents lived in an area of Humanville that headquartered a major corporation. It was very insulated. The corporation controlled the community and its people. Almost everyone worked for the company and was white-collar. I always felt like somebody was watching me, since it was a "big brother" environment. We were taken care of by the corporation, but had to conform to the rules and regulations of the company. It was pretty freaky, actually. One was expected to think and act a particular way, or was ostracized. As a result, I was raised in a "bubble." I had no idea what was going on outside my world. I wanted to know but couldn't break out of the plastic environment I was trapped in. Soooo, I created other outlets for this frustration (which I'll get to in a minute).

Like I told you, I always felt different in some way. Didn't talk about it, I just assumed that maybe, I don't know, I was from another planet or something. I finally realized that the reason for this odd feeling was that I was supposed to become an entertainer and brighten up the world with my talents. *That's* why I was so different than everyone else! This was my quest, and I was going to stop at nothing to achieve it!

Unfortunately, I didn't really have any guidance in my pursuit to "light up the world with my talent," nor did I know *how* to do it …did I want to act, sing, etc.…had no clue. I mean, I faked it a lot and did the old "college production" routine to try to figure it out, but just pretended to know what I was doing. I talked a good game and fooled everyone, including myself, into believing I was destined for stardom. Well, everyone except my parents, who both insisted that the entertainment field was not a valid choice for a career. That's why I moved to a new part of Humanville after college. I fought my way out from under their rule and didn't look back. I was finally free to fly!!! Until, that is, I left the "bubble" of my upbringing and all of a sudden found myself lost in the outer edges of my fair city. Whoa, what a complex, dangerous, and dark place it was! Everything was confusing to me. As I dredged further and further into the heart of the city, I felt the city dredge further and further into my heart. At one point, I could have sworn that I *was* Humanville, and that it breathed through me. I was in way over my head.

You know, now that I think about it, I want to share more about this city of ours. It's not going to be that easy because it's a complicated place. I'm not sure where to begin…or how to do this…hmm…ok…think I've got it.

Let's talk about Humanville…

THE CITY

When I first moved to my new metropolitan home, I was surprised to find out that Humanville was so incredibly huge. In truth, it's the biggest city in the world. It reaches to every corner of the planet. You could not get from one end to the other by jet in an entire day. Even though there are different parts of the city that have different names, they're all suburbs of Humanville. I naively thought that when I left my childhood environment and went to different geographical location, I might be moving out of it. I'd escaped from a small corporate town and gone to a pulsating metropolis, which was in a different region and had a different title, but was shocked to find out I was still in Humanville. As my career grew, I traveled to foreign lands, thinking they would be different, but never could get out of the city. It was amazing! Anywhere I went, I was immersed in it. I was aware that it was big because because I'd studied all about it in school, but guess it didn't really sink in. I finally realized that Humanville was everywhere! There was no escape. Not that I was really trying to because I didn't know I was a prisoner. It was just surprising that the city was so diverse.

If I had to describe Humanville in one word, it would be "intense." I felt a need to match the energy surrounding me just to keep up. I continually got swept away in the challenge of "fitting in" and being what it demanded me to be. (Remember my not so flattering self-description, earlier?)

I once wrote a college essay about Humanville that, in my opinion, pretty well sums it up. I thought, at the time, that I'd been complimentary but thorough. I started out by saying that the city was the most extraordinary place in the world to live. My writing continued with the following description...

"In some areas, it's vibrant and pulsates with energy and excitement. It's home to great restaurants, theatre, culture, art, and entertainment. Also, all business is headquartered in Humanville. It's quite a vision to see how the corporate world operates under the guidelines of the city. You'd think you were watching a well-choreographed war, with each battle carefully plotted and executed. Impressive, to say the least. Then there are areas that seem quite rural and quaint. Even though they appear to be small towns, the fact is, these places are actually more extensions of this vast city."

I covered many aspects of Humanville, but apparently got a little carried away with my thoughts. I went on to say...

"Humanville was founded a very long time ago. Centuries, actually. It became a boomtown early on and has not stopped growing since its inception. There have been many wars fought on Humanville soil, and lives have been lost trying to protect...well, I'm not sure what the reasons were. I'd venture to say that those who fought couldn't answer that question, either. Power struggles have plagued the city throughout time, and it has never actually had a stable political foundation. However, this fact is hidden behind an intense marketing strategy that has been quite successful at presenting Humanville as the worldwide leader in all aspects of life: business, commerce, government, economics, medicine, and science, to name a few. The laws that rule this city were established to control the community, not to serve it fairly and objectively.

Greedy, power-hungry leaders who play negative mind games are at the core of Humanville's chaotic, yet powerful governing machine. Decision-making in the legislative body of the city isn't motivated by the concept of right and wrong...quite the contrary, winning or losing is all that matters. This attitude permeates every aspect of Humanville, making everyday life extremely frustrating. The thought, "I can't get ahead" constantly dwells in the hearts and minds of its people, although no one would ever dream of publicly acknowledging these feelings. It's all about "appearances" and, trust me, nobody forgets that!

Geographically speaking, Humanville is the home to mountains, beaches, deserts, lakes, ocean shores, farmland, etc. Some parts of the city are absolutely beautiful, with well-manicured streets and exquisitely designed buildings, but there are also neighborhoods that aren't as impressive. Those are more hidden, but still have the same community pressure as the upscale areas.

To understand why Humanville is so attractive, we need to go into the sociology of the city. It appeals to a wide variety of people from all walks of life. Scholars, athletes, artists, scientists, doctors, lawyers, housewives, students, and laborers have all lived here. As I've mentioned, Humanville is perceived to be the most impressive city in the world. On the surface, this would appear to be true. People tend to believe that if they think and act a certain way, their lives will be filled with money, success, power, fame, etc...and they're willing to do anything necessary to achieve these goals. The citizens of Humanville make up a competitive community! Nothing is considered out of line when it comes to striving for success.

The thought that one can be happy in Humanville is actually a facade, but a powerful one. It has a subtle way of making people feel unworthy because it advertises what one "should own, should make, should drive," etc. The energy of the city makes people constantly question themselves, while pushing them to look like they "have it all together." For the most part, the community isn't even aware of the underlying negativity that drives Humanville. It sublimely brainwashes everyone into a fear-based mindset that keeps them under its control.

Life here is extremely hard. True feelings are masked and telling lies is common. Also, citizens are very guarded because there is no trust. In fact, this is one of the city's strongest control mechanisms. Any behavior that's not motivated by greed, ego, or anger is construed as "weak."

Humanville is very dangerous. Crime is rampant and it's not unusual to see people lying on the street, completely destitute and homeless. It's so commonplace, most of the citizens of Humanville completely ignore and walk right past these individuals without a second thought. Everyone here is too caught up in his or her own affairs to think about anyone else. That's another one of the ludicrous aspects of Humanville. People are quick to judge other's lives, but are completely oblivious to their own issues and fears. It's easier to think the other person is wrong or misguided, etc. Living in this city gives us a license to turn the other way and see only what we want to see...to close off and hide ourselves so we don't have to take responsibility for our actions."

~

I ended up getting a low grade on my essay. At the time, I was devastated because I thought my work had been excellent, but was told by my professor that I'd said many untrue and unflattering statements about Humanville, and was very close to getting expelled for my lack of loyalty and respect.

Although I didn't realize it then, subconsciously I'd allowed some truth to slip out. I certainly hadn't meant to do that because I was driven to be perfect... and was always competing with my classmates to achieve the highest grades. I ended up re-writing it and changing all the things that made Humanville appear to be a "less than ideal" place to live. When I turned the new version in, my grade went up, but I walked out of class that day with an empty feeling.

You see, I kissed up to my professor, and at the time didn't understand what had really transpired in that essay. I *had* studied about Humanville in school, but unbeknownst to me, much of what was learned was propaganda. We were taught that it was the most powerful, productive, and incredible place in the world. I believed it on the surface, but inside struggled with this. I just wasn't aware of the struggle because of my own fear.

Speaking of my fear, I was a master at hiding it. Similar to everyone I wrote about in my essay, I was extremely afraid of life, but didn't publicly display that fact. I had a secret way of dealing with my fear demons…which leads me to…

MY SECRET

Upbringing is the most important gift or curse we bring with us into adulthood. If we're lucky enough to have fair and supportive guidance, which is unconditionally love-based, we have a good chance of being ahead of the game when we set foot in "grown-up land." Most of us aren't so lucky and have to muddle through a lot of pain and mistakes before we get it together, if we ever do.

I, personally, was one of those people who carried a truckload of issues around with me but didn't realize it. I believed I was on top of everything because I learned, early on, a very effective technique for hiding this "eighteen wheeler" from myself. You see, my security blanket of protection in my teen years was a disease called anorexia, which I developed at twelve. Then, after seven years of this hell, I decided to jump into thirteen years of bulimia. If you've never dealt with any food problems, you might not understand the nightmare created by these diseases. However, if you *have* had struggles with alcohol, drugs, or other addictions, you may grasp the frustration of what it's like to feel hopelessly trapped and afraid. I was dealing with a life-threatening disease, but didn't understand this until it was almost too late to overcome it.

In the beginning, anorexia was an attempt on my part to be in charge of my own life and to be perfect. I had parents who loved me, b   re strict (and in my opinion, controlling), so it was incredible to fin   n which they couldn't force me to do something. By no   power over them. It felt great! Also, I was losi   nt I'd blamed my misery on. The thinner I got, the m   e. In reality, I was just exuding a false confidence b   ol" I held over my body and parents. I started pushing   any normal boundaries because I felt invincible. Most   turned my body into the enemy, and could punish myse   disciplined that I ignored its needs.

It was cool to be able to a   ish so many goals… becoming skinny, pushing myself to unbel   ble limits, and punishing my body for being a part of me. If this sounds crazy, you're right it was, but at the time it made sense to me. Let me explain.

Have you ever had a sense of loathing and hatred about yourself? I would hope not, but unfortunately I did. Anytime we punish ourselves, it's because we don't feel worthy of love. Why not? Well, it's not so hard to figure out. The truth is, the way we were taught to perceive ourselves as children is how we subconsciously perceive ourselves as adults.

In my case, I was part of a family that was solid, but was also living in Humanville. I was a middle child and didn't feel special at all. My parents didn't understand the individual nature of each child's personality. I was very different from my siblings, but we were all grouped into a "unit." I had a rivalry with my older sister. She'd been very rebellious as a young teen and got into a group of friends who abused drugs, stole, lied, skipped class, and who knows what else. She was arrested once but not convicted, and ran away twice, just to be dramatic. Even though her actions were troubled, at least she received attention from my parents (negative attention is still attention). I needed to establish my own way of getting them to notice me, so I overachieved in school and extra-curricular activities. I thought if I was perfect, I'd be special to them and would be praised for my outstanding achievements. Mom and Dad, though, didn't want to show favoritism to any one child. They didn't realize the attention they showed my sister counted because it involved negative situations. Even though this seems fair, in my case, it led to extreme frustration. I desperately desired for them to acknowledge that they were proud of me. Only then could I believe I was truly loved. I never got what I needed, so started to think I was worthless.

They didn't understand, and I didn't know how to fix things. So, I discovered dieting and starvation. It was also my way of punishing them. The more they worried, the more powerful it felt. I was angry with them for not embracing and encouraging me to be anything I wanted to be and acknowledging my accomplishments. I did what I did for *them*, so they'd be proud of me. They never told me they noticed my efforts. I was constantly running into a brick wall. Also, being a risk taker was something they didn't relate to. I perceived life and dreams very differently, so subconsciously bought into the idea that I was bad for having aspirations that were opposite than the life they lived. I was so desperate to have my own identity and driven to break away from their control, though, I fought like hell to defy them in any way possible. The problem was that deep inside I believed that choosing my own direction was wrong, so I had to bury that feeling.

Anorexia gave me false confidence and it carried me through, but life was extremely limited. I created a world that was safe for me. As long as I could keep within my structure, I'd remain skinny and powerful! It was so fragile in reality, but I lived in denial.

I'll give you an example of my normal day. First thing every morning, I'd get up and jump rope for 30 to 45 minutes, then brush my teeth, shower, and dress for class (this was in college). I'd walk to campus, which would get at least one to two miles of exercise in. I'd come back after class and have a lunch that consisted of one slice of low-fat bread (45 calories) with one thin slice of turkey (the kind that has only 20 calories a slice) with mustard, no mayonnaise. Some days I'd substitute a salad that had lettuce, a tomato slice, and no dressing (about 30 calories). This would be the first food I'd eat. Then I'd change into running clothes and go out, no matter what the weather was, and run 9 to 12 miles. Didn't miss a day—well, that's not true. There *were* two days in my junior year of college that I caught the flu. I didn't run those days. After that I'd come back and dress for my extra-curricular activities. I was on heavily involved on campus: student entertainers, student government, varsity revue, theatre, sports…you name it. These activities kept me moving. In the summer, if it was still light outside, I'd come back home, hop on my bicycle and try to get 20 to 30 miles in before dark. In winter, I'd go to the gym and swim 50 to 70 laps. Dinner consisted of one piece of protein (enough for three bites of chicken, turkey, or beef, that, by my calculations, would be about 200 calories), one baked potato (dry—125 calories), and occasionally, an extra steamed vegetable—no butter (not over 25 calories). I'd study in the evening, and end the day with 100 push-ups and 500 sit-ups. That was it. I lived on 400 to 500 calories a day. At one point, I even cut the calories down to about 200 a day (no protein, too fattening). How I survived is beyond me. I did have friends, but was not close to anyone because they came second to my exercise. I also didn't date very much. A man might get too close and that would be very dangerous.

This was my life for seven years. It was a very lonely existence because I isolated myself emotionally and was afraid of intimacy. I had an outgoing personality, so was well liked and popular, but inside knew I was fooling everybody. I thought I was worthless. But, even though I had an anorexic mindset— a deep emptiness within me—I made up for it and felt powerful because I'd conquered the body, the enemy. I wouldn't listen when my body wanted something, like food, because it needed to be punished. I was winning a war most people lost. The more I didn't let my body tell me what it needed, the better I was than everyone else. I was more disciplined and perfect than they were, and therefore, was "special." See how it works?

Absolutely crazy, but what I never got from my environment as a child, I finally achieved by starving myself in my adolescence and young adulthood.

Anorexia is an extremely difficult disease to overcome because the mindset is so locked in warped thinking and doesn't see reality. Even when looking at myself in the mirror, I didn't see a skinny body. I saw one that needed to lose weight here or there, and was never perfect enough. I also didn't trust anyone else's opinion. When someone would tell me I was too thin, my thought was that he or she was jealous. I was keeping weight off, and they couldn't, so they were trying to sabotage me! When you don't trust anyone, you become paranoid and think everyone's out to get you.

Looking at my own features, I wouldn't see thick and long auburn hair or crystal clear, sea-foam colored eyes. Instead, bizarre straw-like horsehair and strange, almost otherworldly eyes that looked alien and frightening would stare back at me. I couldn't bear to look at myself most of the time because there were just flaws...my cheekbones were too high, my nose was too pointy, my neck was too long, and my skin tone didn't match my other features. Every single thing about my physical appearance repulsed me. This repulsion was the driving force behind my disease.

So it went on and on, until the end of my junior year in college. I became anemic and literally couldn't push myself anymore. My body just quit. It couldn't take it. Talk about feeling like a failure!!!! I gained weight and thought I was literally going to die because of my fear of becoming fat. In fact, to me at that time, death would have been a better option. The only thing that kept me from ending it all was the desire not to hurt my parents.

Isn't that ironic!?! The very people I was trying to get back at were the same people I cared enough about to not end my life.

I survived anorexia by falling into a year of extreme overeating. I gained thirty-five pounds and panicked every second. I just couldn't stop! I think my body was so excited about getting food, it just took over. My metabolism was also pretty screwed up at this time, so nothing was working right, really. During my starving years, my body was forced to operate on low caloric intake. It compensated for this by shifting my metabolic rate and as a result, grew accustomed to operating at a very high energy level with little fuel. I'd actually created more of a trap for myself because I had to keep up the intense exercise level to stay thin even with low food intake. The second I was forced to "slow down," my metabolism didn't shift immediately and I started gaining weight, even though I was still only eating 200 to 500 calories a day. I'd also gotten into the habit, by this point, of only eating once a day (early evening), and no other time. My body had to function for twenty-three hours a day without fuel. This didn't help to balance my metabolism. In fact, it led to the overeating. During this panic time, I went from anorexia into bulimia.

Oh, bulimia. This disease was, in some ways, easier to deal with than anorexia because I could be somewhat normal looking, but still have a secret security blanket. It kind of crept up on me as I was trying to control my weight gain after my anorexic experience. I really didn't think I'd become addicted because it seemed manageable to me (oh yeah, right). I started utilizing the behavior when I felt like I'd eaten too much at a meal. I could "get rid of" anything I felt guilty about. Talk about new found power! Now,

I could eat whatever I wanted to, and then not have to deal with the consequences of overeating. The added benefit was that I could go through the process of "burying" a pain or hurt by overeating, and then "purge" not only the food, but also the pain with it. The very act of purging was getting rid of the problem that motivated the eating in the first place. How great was that!?! At first, it seemed to work, but before long I couldn't stop eating even when desiring to because I knew how to get rid of it. Then I became a prisoner. It literally got to the point that I couldn't eat a meal, or anything, without purging it.

There again, I'm not sure how I survived thirteen years of this behavior, purging sometimes as many as fourteen to fifteen times a day. There were brief periods—sometimes weeks, sometimes months—when I didn't practice the disease, but they were short-lived and there was constant fear that it would flair back up again. It always did. My entire existence depended on the ability to eat away my problems, then purge them along with the food I consumed. Thirteen years of this.

You know, this isn't real easy to talk about, but it's necessary to in order to give you a chance to see how I lived in Humanville. Fear completely controlled my life...

I also was extremely naïve, as you already know. I hadn't been exposed to essential growing experiences during my childhood. As a result, insecurity ruled and I gave my power away to others in almost every situation. I didn't feel worthy enough to think I deserved to be treated with love and respect.

This is a very important point to recognize, because my life in Humanville was founded on my lack of self-love (like everyone else who lives here).

My first romance as an adult is a perfect example of this naivety. This happened right after I got out of college. The relationship went something like this...

THE BOYFRIEND

I've just moved to a new part of the city. It's very vibrant, and exciting, and I'm scared to death. I want so desperately to be noticed and be important. How can I pull this off...I want to fit in, but this is going to require a lot of acting. Oh god, there is a man talking to me. He seems very nice, and almost shy. I think he likes me. Oh, geez, he just asked me out. Of course, I accept. He takes me to a beautiful restaurant in the canyon. How romantic!!! He says I'm beautiful...how can I pretend to believe him? I know he's wrong, but I just smile and try to be witty anyway... He does like me! I don't see what he could possibly be attracted to, but he's saying wonderful things to me...Bingo, love match!!

(Three months later). He's spoiling me and buying me all kinds of expensive things, but last night he got upset about something silly, and his anger grew

to the point where his eyes glazed over. He scared me a little, but I managed to calm him by being very sweet. I'm sure he was overreacting because he's under a lot of stress and is about to go through a divorce. I didn't know that he wasn't divorced when we met, but that's ok because I know he loves me, and I'll be very supportive during this time. He did tell me he hit his wife and broke her jaw once, and that was unsettling, but he would never do that to me. I'd never be mean or provoke him like she did...no, of course he'd never do that to me...

(Six months later). Now I'm living with him and he's in the middle of his divorce. He's very angry and feels like he is being attacked. I've never seen divorce before. This is pretty horrible. His moods are growing darker, but I'm sure he didn't really mean to push me that hard yesterday when he took my arm and made me go into the bathroom to see the scale. He told me that he'd gained weight and that it was my fault. Then he pushed me to the floor. I wasn't hurt, really, but got scared. His eyes were glazed again. He called me a cunt and whore. He's done that before, but he seemed to be meaner than he usually is. I hope his divorce is over soon. Then he'll feel better.

(Four months later). I'm presently at my friend's house. I had a little bad luck with my boyfriend. You see, he thought I was thinking about leaving him, so he got mad and threw everything I owned into the pool. He then picked me up and held me over the balcony threatening to drop me, but fortunately changed his mind and instead threw me down and tried to kick me, but lost his balance and missed. He cursed at me, then ran outside and started to roll my car down the hill. He was really mad! I called my friend while he was gone, and luckily, my friend showed up in time to save the car

and help me fish all my things out of the pool. My boyfriend drove off in a rage after threatening to kill us, but I think he was bluffing. Anyway, he just showed up at my friend's house and told me he was going to kill himself if I didn't come home. Guess he really loves me, huh? Can't live without me. I don't know what to do...

(Five months later). I'm back at the house. He was so nice to me after I left to stay at my friend's house, it didn't feel like he'd do anything mean again. I know he loves me. He is so remorseful after he gets in these moods, and is so sweet, giving, and nurturing. I've wanted to be on my own for awhile and try to stand on my own two feet, but he's taken over my finances and says I would never make it on my own. Maybe he's right, it doesn't seem like I can do much of anything right now. I might have to stay here forever. Wish I could say I love him, but I'm too scared to feel that way most of the time. Maybe this is the way life really is... I should just accept this. He doesn't really mean to hurt me, he just gets upset a lot.

(Four months later). I'm packing my things quickly and trying desperately to get out of the house before he returns. I'm so scared right now, and have such little time to get out. He said he would be back in three hours, but he always comes home early. Always. He finally did something today that made me realize I'm going to die if I stay here any longer. We had an argument. This one, like so many others, had been brewing for a couple of days. I knew he was getting upset, but didn't know what was going on in his head, or why he was getting angry. I've adopted the "build up, blow up, make up" terminology to describe the process. I've been through it so many times. This blow up ended with him grabbing a knife and holding it to my

throat and threatening to kill me. I just sat there, completely still, breathing very shallow and trying to look him in the eye. I was scared out of my mind, and truly didn't know if he would do it. Then, for some reason, I took a chance and said, "If you really are going to do this, then do it now. I won't struggle, I'll look you straight in the eyes and you will see I'm not afraid of you." Now, I have no idea why I said that because I was more scared than ever, but it worked because he just hesitated for a second, then sat the knife down and left. He said he would be back in a few hours. For all I know, he went to buy a gun, but I gotta tell you, I'm not waiting around to find out! Oh god, I just hope I can get enough stuff out of here to survive. There's so little time. Where am I going to go? I'll figure that out later. Just have to get out now...

~

You know, I actually did leave the house that day and never moved back in but it took almost two more years to completely break the tie of that relationship. It was so mixed up and confusing, and I had so much fear...it's interesting how a lack of self-love can keep us in bad situations. That relationship was a nightmare for me, but I had to go through it to learn important lessons. I had to be threatened with death to finally stand up for myself and run away. It was my first experience in boundary setting. Ok, so my boundaries were extremely broad. At least in the end I got out alive.

Unfortunately, I continued living in Humanville...

The thing is, though, *everyone* who lives in Humanville has his or her own story of struggle and pain. Every story is unique in description, but not in motivation. We all, in this fair city of ours, have tried to deal with our lives, but have lived in fear. Bottom line... I'm reminded of a sad memory that has stayed with me for years. It's about a family who lived in Humanville and couldn't overcome the pain, and lost the struggle...

JUSTIN'S CAR

I knew a guy in high school whose childhood could not have been more different than mine. He came from a broken home. His parents divorced when he was just a small boy. He *had* been old enough to remember the fights. The horrible, deafening arguments between his mom and dad that usually ended up in a furniture throwing match and, ultimately, physical violence.

Justin's father was a troubled man. He'd shown promise as a young, newly married college sophomore. He'd earned a partial athletic scholarship to a state university and had excelled in football and academics. He worked hard at school, held two part-time jobs to help support he and his wife, and trained twice as hard as any other guy on the team because he planned to "go all the way." He had his eye on the top. He was going to become a pro. He was sure of it.

He married his high school sweetheart. She'd been the homecoming queen of their high school. She worked some to help out and attended class, but didn't plan on finishing college. Why should she? Her husband was going to be rich and famous, and she would be the "adoring, beautiful wife" who would cheer for her man while she sat next to the other wives in the special "designated" seats in the stadium. She'd have a wonderful wardrobe, which would be showy enough to attract the TV cameras to her when the network cut to the players' wives during the games. She planned on doing charity work or something like that. Anything high profile and interesting enough to entice the Humanville elite to support her cause. She'd find a way to create her own recognition.

Unfortunately, two things happened in the same week that changed Justin's parents' lives forever. The first was a terrible injury his dad received during an intense pre-game practice that almost ended his life and definitely his football career—he broke his back while being tackled from behind. The other event of the week was the discovery that Justin's mom was pregnant with him.

You can imagine how overwhelming it was for Justin's parents to deal with all of this. In time, his dad recovered enough to resume a somewhat normal life but was never able to move with much flexibility again. His mother was heartbroken that her dream of being a famous "football wife" had been shattered, but was stuck because she was carrying her husband's baby and had nowhere else to go.

The baby was born, and they struggled to support him. His dad found work as a telemarketer because he didn't have to move around much. His mom waited tables at night after his dad got home and could watch Justin. The problem was, his dad started to get home later and later. In fact, sometimes he wouldn't show up until right before his mom came home from work! Justin would be in his crib, crying for hours...hungry, dirty, and needing to be changed. No one would be there. He was no more than a one-year-old when this started happening. His mother would actually leave before his dad would get home, cursing him for not being there but swearing he wouldn't make her late.

Three guesses where his dad would be...yep, he found comfort for his pain and problems at the local sports bar. He'd given up classes long before because he needed to "get a drink after work" everyday. He couldn't fit studying into a life that was filled with work, a kid, and a nagging wife.

The fights started around this time. They escalated until one day his mom ended up in the hospital, and his dad, in jail. A neighbor watched Justin until the ordeal was over, but before long, it happened again. Neither of his parents took action to change or rectify the situation for three years. They just wallowed in their unhappiness.

Finally, they did split, and Justin found himself being tossed back and forth, the pawn in a power game between the two. His dad still drank, and his mother started dating anybody who'd ask her out. She usually ended up living with them. Justin just tried to survive. He never felt like he had a real home or real love, but he did become tough.

When I met him, he was the coolest guy in school. He was brilliant and street smart. He didn't have a lot of patience for the silly high school stuff like extra-curricular activities or sports (look what it had done for his dad.) He *did* show up for class everyday, though, and was a straight A student. He was a very intense young man, and I could tell that he was determined to make a better life for himself than what he'd been raised in. He would talk about his plans to go to college. He knew he'd have to support himself through this process, but that didn't deter him. He was awarded an academic scholarship, to the surprise of many, and actually showed a little excitement when he found out. Justin was not one who showed much emotion, so I knew he was proud of his accomplishment.

I was most impressed with his ability to focus. No matter what he was doing, he was right there—total concentration. Even in conversation, if he was talking to you, you were the most important thing in Justin's world during that time. He wouldn't look around and his mind would not drift. It was like he was hanging on every word you'd say. Whenever we'd talk, I felt very interesting and important to him. He made everyone feel that way. He was special.

He also worked at the local garage. He loved cars. They were his passion! In fact, he saved his money and bought an incredible one. It was a vintage Porsche that he'd found pretty beat up, and had restored. His car was his life... his image... it reflected him—powerful, sleek, sexy, and dangerous.

Home life was a nightmare, but he endured it. His father would come back drunk most nights and beat the crap out of him if he could find him. Justin usually tried to time it so his dad would be passed out by the time he got home, or he'd just stay out all night if he sensed his dad would be on a rampage. His instincts were exquisite—he'd learned how to read the situation very well by this time. He quit even dealing with his mom because she'd pretty much destroyed her life with her own demons (drugs, bad men choices, alcohol,etc.). He'd been kicked out of her house by the latest boyfriend, and she'd done nothing to stop it.

One night, Justin got home before his dad and decided to just lock himself in his room, hoping his dad would just stagger into his own bedroom and pass out. No such luck. His dad came home in a "bad drunk" and proceeded to break down Justin's door, go in, and beat him. He then grabbed the keys to Justin's car and told him he was taking "the precious baby" for a spin. Justin ran after him, begging him to stop, knowing his dad couldn't drive that car sober, much less drunk. He tried to reach it before his dad took off.

That's when tragedy struck. As Justin ran out into the street to try to stop his dad, his father hit the gas, floored it, and ran over his son. The tires on the right side of the car crushed Justin, killing him instantly. His father was so drunk that he didn't realize what he'd done until he got to the end of the street and the car died. He slowly got out of it, staggered over to something in the street and looked down. He saw his son lying there, dead.

Justin's father never took another drink of alcohol. He was arrested that night, charged with involuntary manslaughter, convicted, and sentenced to twelve years in prison. Shortly after his trial, he hanged himself in his jail cell.

I went to Justin's funeral, and his mother was there with her boyfriend. She didn't even cry. Not one tear. In fact, she almost looked relieved. I wondered if she felt Justin and his father had gotten their "just due" for ruining her life years before. I wouldn't have put it past her...

Justin's family depicted a tragic example of how Humanville can distort what's really important in life. His parents thought that when their goal of fame and fortune had been taken away, life was over and they were worthless. They not only bought into it, they dragged their son into their nightmare and even placed some of the blame for their misery on him. As sad as this story is, it is not so unusual. Humanville history is full of similar tales. It's just not easy in the city...

AS LONG AS IT LOOKS OK...

If I've been a bit "heavy" in my discussion about what life in Humanville is like, I wish I was just being dramatic. Unfortunately, everything I've told you so far is what it's like here. Don't get me wrong, we do have fun in the city and can appear to be happy, because a lot of pain is hidden. Those of us who have spent our lives in Humanville are masters at disguising it. Well...we *think* we are. In reality, it's obvious something's bubbling below the surface, but we imagine no one notices. We can even fool ourselves into believing we are happy, at least in the short run. So we party on, keeping up appearances. Oh, yeah, we do this because we're convinced that we'll be considered "worthless" if we don't look like winners. It's an unbelievable waste of energy.

I could go on and on, because one thing the citizens of Humanville are experts on is wasting energy in the "quest to impress." We get our priorities all confused, and even go to the extreme of blaming others for that confusion when things don't work out.

As I am saying this, I'm chuckling to myself while remembering how many times I've done some extremely foolish things trying to play this little game of show.

Here's one of my better ones...

THE SKI TRIP

Shortly after I'd finished touring with my first major band, I started dating a man who, in my opinion, was the most magnificent creature on the face of the planet. His name was William, and he was the CEO of a major film studio. He was "the catch" of the century and women fell at his feet. He just took all the attention in stride. He was forty-two, single, had a huge estate on the beach, drove my favorite car (a Mercedes convertible), had his own private jet (it was actually the studio plane, but he used it like it was his own), and was even gorgeous. We met at an industry party, and he asked if he could call me. Well, of course I said yes, and he did the next week.

I tried very hard to keep my head together, not wanting to get swept up in a whirlwind romance that might end in heartbreak. In all honesty, I was so trapped in my eating disorder that it would've been impossible for that to happen. However, since I never acknowledged that bulimia prevented me from achieving anything, I assumed I *could* fall in love with this man.

Looking back, I bet what intrigued him most about me was my mysterious nature. I was just trying to hide a part of myself (my insecurities), but I guess my aloofness came across as sensual or something. Whatever it was, he was crazy about me.

He invited me on a ski trip and I jumped at the chance to go with him. I was so excited that I failed to tell him I couldn't ski very well. In fact, I lied and said I adored skiing and had grown up on the slopes. I *had* gone skiing twice before, but had barely gotten past the bunny slopes. I was athletic, but didn't have enough practice in the sport to feel confident about my abilities. Nonetheless, figured I could fake it. I mean, how hard would that be, really? I'd just play the "perfect girlfriend" role a little. Let him go out in the morning with his "buddies" and ski the tough runs (show how understanding I was of the "male-bonding" thing), then meet him for lunch (wearing my incredibly adorable color-coordinated ski suit!) We'd ski a couple of easy runs in the afternoon. Then I'd tell him I didn't want to go up the mountain too high because the altitude might hurt my ears and effect my singing—ok, it was a stretch, but he was a movie guy. What did he know about how sensitive a singer's ears were?

Anyway, what I haven't explained is that Humanville has some of the most outstanding ski mountains in the world, and the most treacherous. Unbeknownst to me, William had arranged a surprise. Since I'd gone on and on about how great of a skier I was, he took it upon himself to set up a "helicopter" ski trip for me. Now, if you don't know what this is, let me tell you, it's the most frightening experience in the world if you don't know what you're doing. A helicopter flies you to the top of a mountain, drops you off, and then you have to ski the entire way down to the bottom. It's not such a big deal for a good skier, somewhat challenging maybe, but feasible. For me, it was a nightmare.

When William "surprised" me with this, it was too late to back out. It was our first day, and we were literally leaving the chalet to head for the slopes, I thought. We walked outside and there was a car waiting for us to take us to the helicopter. What could I say? We hadn't even started our vacation yet, I couldn't tell him that I'd lied!

We got in the car, and I broke out in a cold sweat. By the time we reached the helicopter, I was hyperventilating. I tried not to let my fear show, and guess I succeeded because William mistook my terror for overwhelming joy. He was so proud of himself for giving me such a great surprise!

We got to the top of the mountain and the helicopter dumped us out. There were four other people with us, and everyone got their equipment on and took off down the mountain. I struggled with everything… tightening the ski boots, getting my skies on, etc. I kept losing my balance and getting tangled up in the poles. I told William I was just so excited, it was causing me to hurry too much. Finally, I couldn't stall anymore, so we pushed off. It took me about, oh, I'd say a minute, to take my first fall. I tried to laugh it off, and he stopped to help me up. We took off again. I was going about as fast as a snails pace, you know, cutting real wide and keeping my legs spread apart so I wouldn't go too fast.

William sped past me and stopped about 100 yards down the slope. He yelled, "What's wrong with you? I thought you said you were a good skier!" I yelled back, "Sorry sweetheart. I think my bindings are too loose!" (Yes, still stalling...I didn't know what else to do!) William had to come back up the mountain, doing the "side-step with skies on" walk to get to me. It took him about ten minutes to reach me. I could tell he was getting frustrated. He checked the bindings and of course they were perfect. I thanked him profusely (using the "oh, you big, strong man" thing), smiled sweetly, and said, "Ok, let's go!"

At that very moment, I knew I was in trouble. I was just going to have to go for it, and hope that somehow, someway, I'd make it to the bottom of that mountain! I stood tall, angled my skies, looked William straight in the eye and said very provocatively, "See you at the bottom, big boy." I dug my poles into the snow, and with one mighty push, off I went...

I was flying! I didn't even see William after about thirty seconds. Since I didn't know what I was doing, I wasn't cutting at all, but was just a missile shooting down the mountain. For a brief instant, I actually thought I was going to be able to pull it off. In fact, this was even fun! I felt invincible, and free, and ...uh oh!!! That's when it happened. I must have hit something, because all of a sudden, I had no balance. I fought with myself, trying to stay upright, using my poles. Unfortunately, I was going so fast that the poles were actually a deterrent. They kind of stuck in the ground, causing me to lose my balance and fall. However, I didn't stop, but kept going as fast as I'd been on my skies, only now I was on my back, no, my side, no my stomach...I was careening out of control! I zoomed by the other skiers, who scrambled to get out of my way. Everything was a blur to me, so I didn't even know I almost took them out. All I could do was hope that somehow I would stop, eventually. I knew I was in a dangerous situation, but didn't really have time to think about just how dangerous it was. It happened too fast.

All of a sudden, I was airborne. I knew this was bad. Fortunately, I was only afloat for a second before hitting an embankment of very deep snow that stopped me, cold. I lay there for a few seconds, doing a mental check to see if, first, I was still alive. Then I went over every body part, and realized that my left ankle didn't feel right. Not bad, considering I should've died, really. I'd lost my skies somewhere along the way, and had torn my ski suit. (Damn, it had been expensive!) Anyway, I struggled to get up out of the snow. My ankle was killing me, but at least I managed to turn over and face upward instead of down. That's when I understood what had happened.

Apparently, I'd gone off the side of a cliff, but fortunately landed on a ledge that was about ten feet below. The snow was so deep it had broken my fall. How lucky was I!?! I couldn't believe it. Wow, what a ride! I almost laughed out loud, I was so thankful to be alive. I mean, if that ledge hadn't been there...I couldn't think about that.

Just then, William's head poked out over the cliff I'd flown over. By the horrified look on his face, I realized that he thought I'd careened to my death. The second he saw me, the look of horror changed into a look of relief (which I thought was a good sign). He yelled down and asked if I was all right. I answered that I might have hurt my ankle, but was otherwise ok. As soon as he heard that, the look on his face shifted into something that resembled either anger or disgust (I couldn't tell which). What I *could* tell was that he was *not* happy!

As it turned out, one of the other people with us had to ski down to the bottom of the mountain to get help. The ski patrol had to use a helicopter to rescue me because I was still near the top of the peak. I ended up severely spraining my ankle, but not breaking it. It was a relief when I heard that, but it took just as long to heal from the sprain.

William was a little upset with me—ok, that's putting it mildly. Actually, he was furious with me for not telling the truth. In fact, he never forgave me. He said if I could lie about something as benign as skiing, no telling what else I was capable of lying about. I tried to explain that I really wasn't a compulsive liar, I just didn't want to disappoint him. He replied that he was more disappointed in me because of this than he ever would have been if I'd just been honest with him. He even said that he would've gone somewhere else with me if he'd known that I wasn't a good skier. (Now he tells me!)

Needless to say, I never dated William again. When we returned from the trip, he did the "I'll call you soon" routine, but I knew he wouldn't. He wasn't very sympathetic about my injury, either. I think he figured I was so lucky, I deserved a little discomfort, just for good measure. He was probably right. On top of everything else, I had to be on crutches for six weeks. No exercise! I was miserable. (Although I did finally figure out how to run on them...got up to 1 ½ miles a day...kind of had to do a "skip-hop"...not bad, huh? Nothing can stop the will to burn calories!) The whole experience was a disaster, and I'd really blown it!

See what kind of trouble "trying to impress" can get you into? There are a lot of stories similar to the last one. I've made so many ridiculous choices trying to "fit in" and "make an impression." You'd think I'd learn after that, but I didn't. It took me a long time to finally come out of the fog.

Now that I've covered foolish behavior...

THE STRUGGLE CONTINUES

I mentioned earlier that I thought my destiny was to become a performer. Specifically, I ended up deciding to pursue a career in music. I was a very good singer and wrote songs (albeit, not great songs, but my belief was that they had potential), so I started the long process of becoming successful in the music industry. If you know *anything* about this industry at all, you'll understand when I say it's a crapshoot, at best. There's absolutely no secure game plan that will lead you to victory. Talent definitely plays a role, but a surprisingly small role, as it turns out. That being said, I think one of my biggest challenges was trying to find belief in myself. Since I didn't have any, how I achieved *anything* was amazing because I was scared to death all the time. Being a model Humanville citizen, I was continually motivated by a fear of failing. Nothing else mattered than becoming famous to justify my existence.

You can imagine how overwhelming it is to put that kind of pressure on yourself when you're in an industry that has so many variables out of your control. I worked hard and had some cool things happen, but the price I paid in stress and worry outweighed any success achieved. Nothing was good enough. I couldn't see the positive because I focused on the negative. Oh, yeah, I also compared myself to everyone around me. That's always a smart thing to do when you're insecure already.

I don't have to mention that the music industry (like many others, I bet) doesn't give much back. It takes your sweat and soul, sucks you dry, and then laughs as it watches you wither to the ground—then turns and skips away, not looking back, as you shrivel up and die. Does that sound harsh? Well, in Humanville, it's a fact of life.

After many years of dealing with the never-ending pursuit of the brass ring, I found myself at a crossroads. This was motivated by a few hard knocks. I was up for a background singing position for a major tour, but didn't get the gig because they already had a girl with my hair color in the band. (Can you believe that!?!) Then, a very renowned producer who I'd been working with told me he'd have to postpone our project because he'd been hired by a major star to produce *her* album. I'd have to wait. Since I'd just done background vocals on a huge album that was getting a lot of hype, I needed to strike while the iron was hot. When these opportunities fell through, it was so infuriating!

I just got exhausted fighting the battle. The city was consuming me, and I felt like my life had fallen into an abyss. Oh yeah, I was also single during this time, having recently broken up with a man I thought I was going to marry (well, actually, he broke it off). I'd put all of my self-worth into that relationship, so when it fell apart, so did I. My heart was devastated over this loss. The bulimia was way out of control, and overall, I just didn't know what to do.

I was, however, still trying to keep up appearances with my group of friends. As I've told you, some were very influential, high profile, and powerful people. I didn't want to look weak to them, so didn't talk about my disappointments. I maintained my cool, fun, somewhat aloof demeanor, and they never suspected I was in a tough place. To be honest, I don't know if any of them would have truly cared, but I didn't want to risk embarrassment, or worse, judgement from them. It was an extremely difficult time.

Then, the most extraordinary thing happened. The day after the infamous "girl's night out" (that ended at the police station…remember?), I was suffering from a hangover, made worse by taking a sleeping pill on top of liquor. I was depressed, frustrated, hopeless, feeling very sorry for myself, and was basically being a bitch. Ohhh, you're curious now, huh? Well, see for yourself, although I warn you it's not pretty…

EAVESDROPPING...

I'm so exhausted today. I haven't been sleeping at all, lately, and last night didn't help. I don't know what the hell I'm doing or what the hell I'm going to do. I've been in this damn city so long, I think I've been swallowed up by it. I don't even know who I am anymore... Shit. This isn't living. I'm so fricking lonely! Nothing is working...

God, I'm in a bad mood...I feel like ramming the car in front of me just because it's going too slow! I seriously have to fight myself from doing this. I am out of control! Ok, calm down...I think the only thing I want right now is a cup of coffee. Oh geez, I have to go into that fucking trendy coffee shop. I hate those places! I am not in the mood to be stared at because I'm sitting alone. I feel like such a loser. I know, I'll grab a paper on the way in so I'll look like I'm busy...who am I kidding? I'll look like a loser who is trying to look like she's busy. Who cares? I just want a cup of coffee. My god, every single thing I do is bringing on stress, even trying to buy a simple damn cup of coffee!

I need to just park the car and calmly go inside...shit! I just locked my keys in the fucking car! How did I do that? I can't believe I was that stupid! Forget it, damn it, I'll worry about that after I get my coffee. God!!!

Ok, come on, I've got to pull it together...just go inside...cool, there's a table in the corner. I'll grab it. It's kind of close to the next table, but the two people sitting there are so engrossed in conversation, they won't even notice I exist. I forgot to get a paper...shit! All right, I know, I'll get a note pad out of my purse and pretend to be writing a song lyric. That'll work...Umm, I'll doodle a little... I'm really close to the next table... I can totally overhear their conversation...what are they talking about? I can't help but notice how attractive they both are. Not that they're physically beautiful, necessarily, but both of them seem to...glow, or something. It's kind of bizarre. I shouldn't listen to what they're saying, but what the hell, they don't know that I am. I'll keep my head down. They keep talking about their "town." They seem to be from the same place. I've never heard of it...I wonder if it's a suburb of Humanville? I find that hard to believe because I've traveled a lot...that's one good thing about being a singer, I've seen the world. Where are they talking about? They're discussing how everything is so colorful and joyous, and people are full of love and nurturing. They're sharing experiences of gracious giving and of what they refer to as miracles. One of them is talking about how everything there is positive, not negative. Wow, this place sounds pretty amazing. They both are so excited about their home, and there seems to be such a, I don't know, peace about them.

Now they're talking about how fortunate they are to have found Godtown. Godtown? What and where the hell is Godtown? I'm sure I've never heard of this place. Is this some religious cult thing? Oh geez, no wonder they seem weird...no, for some reason I don't think that's true. Oh shit, I just spilled my coffee all over the table because I was leaning in too far to hear what they were saying! Oh no, it's all over my pants. It's still pretty hot, too! Ok, this is not cool...oh, they're looking at me. I just giggle with embarrassment and mumble, "my bad." One of them is offering a napkin. I take it from him, say I'm fine, and thank him for his kindness. He smiles back at me with this amazing smile. There is definitely something different about these two people. I should ask them about the place they've been talking about, but then they'll know I was eavesdropping. They seem to want to talk to me for a couple of minutes. I'm enchanted, but am having a little problem focusing on the conversation because I'm drenched in coffee. They don't seem to mind my appearance. Extremely nice people... interesting.

They kindly end our conversation and then get up to leave. They ask again if I'm ok, and I mutter something ridiculous about wanting to dye these pants black anyway. They laugh and say good-bye. I'm left sitting in coffee with this dumbstruck look on my face. Godtown...hmm, I have to find out more about this place...

~

Well, that night I couldn't sleep again, but this time it was because it felt like a little light had been turned on in my mind. I had no idea what it was, but the more I thought about the conversation I'd overheard, the more I wanted to investigate this so-called "Godtown." It was such a bizarre name. It reminded me of a religious theme park or something. The whole idea seemed silly to me, but for some reason I couldn't help but think there was more to it than that. Now, don't get me wrong. I'd been aware of religion in Humanville. In fact, there was a lot of religion in the city, but I'd always been turned off by the "performance" factor. It seemed to me that people who partook of religion did so because they were expected to, and had no clue what it was really about. Even *I* had been a part of a group that did a lot of music "worship," as they called it, but it was so empty for me. I was playing a part. We were going through the motions, all of us, to make ourselves feel better about screwing up so much and being afraid of so many things. It got to the point where I was uncomfortable in the group. It became competitive because everyone wanted the solo parts, and I constantly felt judged. I was also judging others and was just as competitive as everybody else. That's the way everyone was in Humanville, so I didn't stick out or anything. It's just, it never seemed right, or good, or fulfilling. Nothing ever did, so why should this be any different?

But, Godtown. I was intrigued. I made up my mind to try to do some investigation to find out more about this mysterious place. I finally went to sleep with a new feeling... hope. I hadn't felt that in a very long time...

SEARCHING...

The next day was the start of my quest. I had no idea where to look or who to ask for answers. My computer was being fixed and I didn't have access to it, so the library was my first destination. I looked up everything I could think of that might lead me to some knowledge about this so-called "amazing" town, but came up dry. How could it be that there wasn't *one* bit of information? I mean, even if it was a cult, wouldn't there be some literature? You know, talking about how they worshiped something crazy like, I don't know, pinecones or something. There wasn't one word about this place. I finally gave up and headed back to the coffee shop in hopes of finding the two people that were there the day before. I bought coffee after coffee, two lattes, an expresso, then a cappuccino. After becoming completely wired—absolutely bouncing off the walls—I decided they weren't going to show, and went home feeling depressed.

Every day that week I went back to the coffee shop, but never saw them again. I really didn't know why I became so obsessed in finding out more, but was driven with a burning need to find this place!

You see, something had hit me that day. These two people had been glowing. I saw it just as clearly as I can see my hands typing these words. When they spoke, a little spark of light flew off them and landed on me. That was all it took for me to want more of what they had. Although I didn't realize it, I'd received a glimmer of love, and it had been given to me in such a simple gesture.

The thing is, I was looking for the answers in the wrong place. I was *way* off! As you're about to see, time marched on and I became totally disillusioned. The feeling of hopelessness crept back into my heart and I felt myself slip back into despair...

~

I'm so bummed! I have been, for weeks now, researching and researching, but have not found anything about this "Godtown" place. I'm beginning to think I made the whole thing up. I haven't seen the two glowing people, and I've gone back to the coffee shop every day. If I never drink another cappuccino again in my entire life, it will still be too soon. I'm about to give up. I'm so pissed off! Here I thought this "Godtown" was going to be the answer to all my problems, but the searching is totally stressing me out! I'm more confused now than I was before I ever heard about it. I don't even think there is a "God," much less a "Godtown." I've never bought into all the jargon about God anyway, but my hope was that somehow life could be a little easier. I must be wrong. In fact, I must be wrong about everything!

I'm driving through this city feeling like it's going to consume me. Maybe that's the way it is supposed to be, after all. I've been naïve, dumb, and have been taken advantage of time after time. Life has disappointed me, men have disappointed me, my career has disappointed me, and my family doesn't understand me. I've been trapped in absolute hell for years because even something as simple as eating a meal is a nightmare for me! Every time I try to eat, I end up going out of control and hurting myself. I can't stop, but I can't continue living like this. I'm in a prison and can't find a way to escape. I don't think I can continue living, period...I'm terribly scared and alone! Oh shit, I'm crying and can't see where I'm going. I'll pull into this park. I have got to get out of this car before it runs off the road...yes, that would end it all, wouldn't it, solve everything. I have to think first, I guess. Oh god, I'm so confused!...

Ok...open the door, get out of the car. I just have to get over to that bench. My eyes are burning and of course I don't have a tissue...figures...ok, dry it up. I've got to pull it together ...I can't seem to do it this time...I've never felt as hopeless as I do right at this moment...could I end it all? It's so tempting to think I could...this is just all too hard...I'm rocking back and forth on this bench, crying my eyes out like a crazy person...oh, god, my heart hurts so much...damn it, I'm not alone! There's an old woman in the park with me. I cannot believe she's heading my direction. Can she not see I'm having a breakdown here and just want to be left alone!?! Shit, she's actually going to sit down right beside me. I can't believe this! She's

*staring at me. I'm trying to ignore her, but that's pretty impossible to do...
she's reaching her hand out toward me...ok, this is weird. I can barely see
her because I'm crying so hard and...whoa, she's holding my hand! This is
freaky!! I'm scared...no, wait, I'm not scared. Her hand feels warm...and
gentle. I try to look at her through my watery eyes and focus clearly enough
to see her face. I take in a sharp breath. She's glowing! Just like the
people in the coffee shop! We sit there in silence for a minute, and then she
gets up and leaves. I start to speak and ask her not to go, but for some
reason, can't form the words. I just watch her walk away while I hold my
hand out in the same position that she let go of it, suspended in the air, palm
facing up. I'm awe-struck...*

*My eyes follow her until she's gone, and just as I'm about to gather my wits
to get up, I look down and there (where she had been sitting) is a book. I
pick it up. On the cover, it says "The Godtown Guideline Handbook." My
heart skips a beat, and my hands are shaking. Is this what the people in the
coffee shop referred to as a "miracle?" I just stare at it for a very long
time, then finally gather my courage and slowly open the cover. I peer at
the first page. It's completely blank except for one word that's printed in
small letters. I read it again and again, and am confused. The only word
on the page is "listen"...*

LISTEN...

I sat in total silence for what seemed to be hours. It was probably only a few minutes, but I was overwhelmed with confusion and perplexed by what had just happened. I finally got up, tucked the book under my arm, and made my way to the car. I drove home in a daze. "Listen." That's what the book said. One word! I was *so* disappointed because I had no idea what this meant and had so desperately wanted my questions to be answered.

Listen...to what, or who? I sank into an even deeper depression than I'd been in at the park. After getting home, I threw the book on the dresser and fell on my bed in exhaustion. I couldn't sleep, though, because I was past the point of tired. I tried everything, but there was a war going on in my head. If you've ever attended a very crowded concert and have been surrounded by extreme yelling and talking, you can relate to what was going on in my mind. I wanted it to quit, but there were too many thoughts twisting and turning through my head. I really thought I'd finally gone insane!

The moment I couldn't take any more, I heard what sounded like a whisper calling my name. It was strange that something as quiet as a whisper could be heard through all the frenetic noise, but it was there. In fact, it grew louder and clearer as I focused in on it. Finally, I got close enough to answer back.

I asked what it was, and it replied, "I have been waiting for you."

I inquired, "You've been waiting for me?"

The whisper said, "Yes."

I asked, "Why?"

The whisper answered, "Because I love you."

I thought, "uh oh, what's going on here?"

The whisper responded, even though I didn't mean for it to. It said, "I have always been with you, Desmond, but you have always resisted me and have never listened to my guidance."

Whoa, hold on… the whisper had said, "listen"… that word! I sat up with a start and really focused in on this voice. There was something familiar about the energy of this whisper, but it was a very, very hazy memory.

I decided to continue to talk to it. "Wait a minute. I don't know who you are, or what you are. Of course I'm resistant! This is frightening and crazy, feeling something else going on inside me. Are you telling me I've just ignored you?"

"Yes," it said. "That's been the problem—you have ignored me and never trusted me."

I asked, "Who *are* you?"

The voice responded, "I am the voice of love."

"Oh shit!" I exclaimed, "I really <u>am</u> going crazy! What's going on here?"

It answered, "No, Desmond, you are finally at a point where you have to listen. You have nowhere left to turn but to me. I have been waiting for you. I have always been here."

I became defensive and guarded. "Why have I not heard you before now?"

It said, "Because you haven't listened. You have to choose me, and want to listen. You've always wanted to do things your own way, and try to control."

"Well, tell me, if you've always been here with me, why have I never felt love?" I asked.

It said, "Because you have never invited love into your life. You have lived your life through fear."

Well, the voice *did* have a point. I'd spent my life worrying about everything and being so afraid that I'd stagnated myself over and over again. But hey, I lived in Humanville and was no different than anyone else. In fact, people all around me were guarded and cautious. Why was this voice thing singling me out?

I asked, and it said, "Because you have finally singled *me* out. You came looking for me. You are finally on your knees and can't find help from the outside. You have to look inside for your answers."

I got angry. "Look, I don't know what you're talking about. I'm utterly confused and frustrated. I don't have any answers."

The voice responded, "You have all the answers right here, with me. All you have to do is ask and be open to listening to what I say to you. Listen to the guidelines."

"What guidelines?" I snapped back.

It said, "The guidelines of Godtown."

I actually laughed at this and blurted out, "Oh yeah, right. I have, in my possession, a copy of this so-called *Godtown Guideline Handbook*. It only says one word. A word that doesn't make sense to me."

The voice instructed, "Go get the book you are referring to."

I went and got it. "Open it up to the first page. What do you see?"

I opened the book and almost dropped it when I saw, staring back at me, a total documentation of the entire conversation I'd just had with this voice. I was shocked!

What was going on? It was unreal because I wasn't afraid, but thought I should be. In some ways, something was shifting inside of me, and all I wanted to do was to continue talking to this voice, even though I found the whole experience unsettling and bizarre.

I literally spent the next five hours talking to it and asking all kinds of questions. Every time I took a break from the conversation, I'd return to find it waiting for me. It was patient and loving, and for some reason, felt safe. I'd look in the guideline book during these breaks, and our conversation would be there...every word of it.

It's probably a good time to mention that I wasn't necessarily open to this voice thing. I was having a interesting experience with it but was very skeptical and guarded. I didn't run, though.

(I don't know if I'm describing this very clearly. How can I help you relate to what it felt like? I know...have you ever been in a situation and a feeling inside of you makes you not do something? For instance, you're driving home and usually take a familiar route until one day, for some reason, you intuitively decide to go another way. You don't really know why, but you choose an alternate path. Later, you find out that a major cable on the bridge you always go over broke and caused a severe twenty-car pile up. Why didn't you go that route this time? What made you go another direction? A faint whisper, maybe, that you barely heard but listened to subconsciously. That's what this voice thing felt like, except it was right up front and could be heard loud and clear...hopefully that helps a little.)

Anyway, what's most interesting was the fact that this "voice" knew me in a very pure way, and continuously gave me answers that were logical and unbelievably loving. For instance, here's an example of something that really reached out and touched me...

YOU MEAN *I* HAVE TO UNDERSTAND?

As you know, I was very angry with my parents and was drowning in my eating disorders. I decided to make the voice explain why I was born to a mother and father who were so different from me. I was ready for an argument because I blamed them for all my suffering. The voice diffused my anger immediately. When I asked this question, my answer was...

Voice: Gene pool. Your parents possess all the qualities I wanted for you, so you would be equipped to do what I need you to do. They have their own struggles, but have given you many things that have molded you into the beautiful person you are. That was part of their purpose.

Me: But they're so negative. I never felt like they've truly understood or supported me in my efforts. I still have to battle with them constantly.

Voice: The word is "understand." The path you have chosen is outside their world. They have never been exposed to the entertainment industry or much of the environment in which you live, but you have expected them to grasp all aspects of your life. You are the one without the understanding. They do love you, and have always been there when you really needed them. You need to forgive and love them. Get rid of your anger. It is time.

Well, it had never dawned on me that *I* contributed to the problem at all. I'd always felt like the victim with them, but apparently was really throwing a lot of judgement *their* way because I didn't accept them for being who *they* were. Also, the fact that I was their daughter because they gave me qualities to help fulfill my purpose (whatever that was) just, I don't know, made a deep impression on me.

~

I need to tell you that as unbelievable as it seems, when this voice started talking to me, I was so wrapped up with the novelty of it that I completely forgot to ask about Godtown. I actually had been conversing with it for a couple of weeks when the subject finally came up. I'd covered so many topics and the answers I'd received were so positive and love-based, but at times I'd get defensive because it was so foreign for me to look at the world through loving eyes. When I was in these "angry" moods, I'd usually react in a negative way. When I finally did ask about Godtown, I was defiant and really bitchy, basically demeaning it. In truth, it was my way of protecting myself because I was afraid to find out it might be a place I'd never get to be involved with, since I thought of myself as worthless, etc. So, little miss bitch posed her question like this...

Me: This Godtown place. What the hell is it, where is it, and why have I never heard of it before? I don't even think it's a real town, and maybe I'm involved with some cult-like situation, considering I'm now talking to a strange voice in my head (the drama queen took over at this point). In fact, I might be making all of this up, and this guideline book thing, well, I can't explain that, but maybe I'm really stepping into an evil, dark situation. What's going on here? (I was rather proud of my performance, because now this voice would have to be on the defensive, and I'd "win.")

The voice, in a very calm, loving way, answered me.

Voice: Oh, Desmond, you are so afraid. I will tell you that as long as fear controls your actions and words, you are right, you will never get to be involved with Godtown. I am not saying you will be punished for your fear because that is not how it works. You have the ability to choose love in every situation, and when you finally believe this, and start living this, you will start to understand about Godtown. It is a very real and wonderful place that you *can* reach. You have the power to do so. I also need to tell you that this "cult," as you describe it, is not where you are headed. It is actually where you have been. You have lived in the dark cult of fear. If you define a "cult" as a situation or environment that controls one's thoughts and actions and brainwashes someone into believing he or she no personal power, then you define "fear." It is a huge cult and has many, many followers. You have been a member for most of your life. You just didn't realize it.

Whoa, did that explanation slap me in the face. Because of my mood, I guess I wasn't ready to hear that. I immediately quit the conversation and tried to shake off the image of myself living in a cult. This really bothered me. A wave of fear hit. I equated the word *cult* to evil, and panicked because I thought the voice was lying to me. Maybe it was trying to trick me! I was confused. How could I be living in a cult? It had to be wrong.

My reaction was so typical of a fear-based person. I immediately ran. Shut the door quickly. Didn't want to know the truth. I only knew how to live my life in one way. Although I subconsciously was aware it didn't work, I was terrified to be open to another way of living. It was also frightening because I'd have to honestly look at myself, and was sure I'd be repulsed by what I saw. I did want to unlock the door to my soul, but at this point I was just peering through the peephole, not even reaching for the key.

I stepped back in panic and decided to not have another conversation with my weird little voice. This was all getting a little too close for comfort. I shut it down and dove back into Humanville, thinking I'd be perfectly content with my life the way it had always been...

TROUBLE IN THE CITY

As I went through the next few months, I tried to forget about my bizarre experience by jumping back into my career pursuit and getting involved in a new relationship. I felt like I had a handle on things again. I was plotting out my game plan for music and was meeting with powerful "players" in the industry who were telling me exactly what I wanted to hear. I was taking the bull by the horns, and it felt great! A renowned manager was very interested in working with me and was pouring money into my project. Also, a music publisher offered me a songwriting deal and I signed it, immediately. I felt secure, finally, and thought it was only a matter of time before a record contract would be in my hands.

I also met an incredible man who was everything I needed. His name was Daniel. This successful Humanville entrepreneur was suave, well traveled, and absolutely gorgeous! My perfect match. We made a stunning couple, and certainly turned heads when we entered a room. (Remember the importance of *image* in my industry?) We became involved pretty quickly, and I was complete.

During this period of time, bulimia was still in my life, but I naively thought that it was close to being gone. Oh yeah, sure...actually, I pretended to have it under control, sort of. In all honesty, I was fooling myself because every meal was still a battle...and I always lost.

Every time I sat down to eat, a war was fought in my brain that went something like this...

Ok, I'll have one roll and then have half of my salad, dressing on the side. I'll eat just enough of my dinner to get full, and leave some on my plate. Oh, wow, the rolls are really good. I'll have one more, then not eat my salad. The food is taking a long time to get here. I'm really hungry, so what the hell, I'll have a couple more rolls, then just get rid of it before the meal. Oh god, don't do that! I'm doing so well, but can't sit here and not want to reach out and eat the entire basket of rolls. Just one more. Oh god, I shouldn't have eaten that roll! Oh, shit. What the hell? I've already blown it so I'll just eat everything and get rid of it. I don't want to do that, but have no choice now because it's too late. It won't hurt me to do it just one more time. Oh boy, I'm out of control...I wonder if anyone at the table notices how much I am eating? Maybe, if they do, they just think that I'm one of those people with a fast metabolism that can eat anything. Shit. I hate this, but can't stop. I'm trying to keep up with the conversation, but can't think of anything past finding a polite time to excuse myself to go to the ladies room. I feel like I am going to explode! Ok, I can leave now...Oh no, there's a line, and I have to wait! This is not good. It's crowded in here and someone might know what I'm doing. I don't care, there's no other choice. Oh my god, a woman who's at the same dinner party I'm attending just walked into the ladies room! She came with a friend of Daniel's. She must have followed me in here. I can't ignore her—have to talk to her. I'm trying to be cool and friendly, but am so panicked about getting rid of everything I just ate, I'm sure it shows. I'm afraid she's going to notice what I'm up to. God, what to do? I could procrastinate and maybe she'll leave, but I can't wait much longer. This is bad. I'll just have to hope she doesn't notice...

Ok, I feel so much better now, but she's still in here! What if she saw me and goes and tells her date? He might tell Daniel and my secret would be exposed. I can't let that happen! I'll just freshen up, act very cool, brush my teeth, and say I'll see her back at the table. I look kind of pale and my eyes are watery. Shit, I don't look right. I was so panicky and wasn't careful, so my eyes became teary. Oh god, somebody is going to notice! Act cool. Just sit back down. Good, no one really noticed me come back. Whew, now if that woman doesn't look at me funny when she returns, then everything will be all right, I think. Here she comes. She does look at me, but I don't think she really knows what I just did. Oh man, maybe she does! No, she's acting normal. I hope the color has returned to my face. That was a close call. Ok, that's it. I'm never going to do it again. I can control this!

~

Obviously, that one was lost. The truth is, it was the same scenario at every meal, and I'd declare never do it again each time. Of course, I'd turn around and repeat the pattern immediately. Whether dining out or eating at home, I was always on a sinking ship—not to mention the times I was alone and had to face whatever was bothering me. There was always something that would push me into the behavior. Every single day. Sometimes, as I have mentioned, it would be as many as fifteen or sixteen times in a twelve-hour period. If it seems unbelievable to you, trust me, looking back, it does to me, too. I was so lost in my fear and lost in the disease, but was unaware of how crippling bulimia was in my life. I thought I was handling my secret very well.

At this particular time, I was going through the war mainly at mealtimes, which for me meant the disease was practically nonexistent. Two or three times a day. I'd become such an expert at hiding it, I'm not sure Daniel ever did find out, but there's no way he could get to know who I really was. I had so many walls up and wouldn't let him in any further than what was "safe" to protect my secret. Luckily, he lived in Humanville too, and didn't desire real intimacy. We actually stayed involved for a while.

That being said, the relationship was a huge roller-coaster ride because no matter what he did, I punished and blamed myself for it. For instance, if he became distant and put up emotional barriers (which, as every woman knows, is what guys do from time to time), I'd immediately assume it was my fault because I must have upset him (must punish myself...I'm worthless). Or, he'd be amorous and want to be close to me. I wouldn't respect him because if he was stupid enough to be attracted to me, he must be an idiot, and therefore not worthy of my affections. (My eating disorder personality was in total contradiction at all times.)

I put so much energy into thinking our relationship was real. It's so sad really, because I tormented myself constantly about whether he'd leave me or not. Of course, he eventually did. That's when my life in Humanville finally unraveled...

OH GOD, WHAT HAD I DONE!?!

After I put an end to the "weird voice" experience, I thought my life had finally come together. This was totally delusional, but life in Humanville always is, so I really believed things were turning around— that is, until Daniel broke up with me. No need for any more explanation about why that happened! My fragile world started to fall apart. I was devastated over losing him and went into a depression. Also, as luck would have it, my publishing deal ended right before my eyes, and there was nothing I could do about it. The company, an independent corporation, lost its funding and had to drop all of its songwriters. I was thrown out on the street without warning. It was unbelievable!

I was heartbroken, lost, and had nowhere to turn. Except —you guessed it— to my security blanket...my disease. I needed to bury the pain, and there was no better way. I fell into a dark hole that I couldn't crawl out of—I could not quit, and did not want to quit, bingeing and purging, burying the pain and disappointment. Over and over and over, I didn't care…just had to stop hurting!!! This lasted for many days, until something happened that finally *did* stop me, but not in the way you might think.

When you put that much physical strain on yourself, it becomes a very dangerous situation. Not only does it slowly destroy the body, it also upsets your electrolytes, causing you to short-circuit. In other words, you can have a heart attack and die in an instant. I'd been through a couple of close calls before, but what happened that day made the other times pale in comparison.

After one particularly taxing session, I suddenly felt very hot and started perspiring profusely. At the same moment, I felt a very sharp pain in my chest on the left side, and my left arm went numb. I lost control of my body and fell to the floor. There was a shooting pain in my jaw, then my heart started beating so quickly I thought it was going to jump out of my skin! At this moment, I knew I'd finally punished myself to the point of having a heart attack—I was about to be killed, and it was my own fault! I'd caused this to happen and was now facing the consequences! I was extremely scared but couldn't get help because I was alone. I was going to die and no one would know about it for days at least—maybe longer, because I had isolated myself so I could binge and purge! My friends had left me alone, figuring I was depressed and needed some time to get over my sadness.

My heart was beating faster and faster, and my chest was in excruciating pain! I didn't want to die! I really didn't mean for this to happen, I just didn't want to hurt anymore, and didn't want to feel pain. *That* was why I'd gone on this rampage, not to kill myself. Oh god, what had I done!?!

Through the pain, I started thinking about my parents, my siblings, and their children. I didn't want to leave them! I thought of my friends and how much everyone meant to me. I was in agony and knew I was running out of time...

The very second my heart was about to explode and stop, I heard the whisper...the voice...through the pain...through the fear...calling to me...telling me it loved me and could help me. I asked for its help...I pleaded to it... begged it to make the pain stop...to please calm my racing heart!

I heard it say, "Trust Me, Desmond. I am here for you always, and I do love you. You can stop the pain by forgiving yourself right now. You are worthy of loving yourself. You can choose to live, or you can choose to die. It is within your power. Love your body, and understand you and your body are one. It loves you, and doesn't want to fail you. Tell your body you love it."

At this very moment, a miracle was given to me. I said out loud, "I love you...I love you...I love you!" and the pain immediately ceased, and my heart slowed down. I came to my senses and found myself on the floor, drenched in sweat. The feeling slowly returned to my arm and my heartbeat returned to normal. As I calmed down, I heard the voice loud and clear.

It said, "You have just been given a gift, and you have a purpose to fulfill here. It is time you open your heart, embrace love and let go of your fear. Love is the most powerful force in the universe. It is the life-giver, and the miracle-maker. You have just experienced love in action. Be thankful for your lesson, for you are blessed."

I stayed where I was for a few minutes, then slowly sat up and leaned against the wall. As my breathing returned to normal, I closed my eyes and started crying. I knew I'd almost just died, and the tears were the acknowledgment of my sorrow and also of my relief. Something dangerous had occurred, and I'd been lucky…but it was more than luck. I'd been blessed, and something greater than I could imagine had saved me. I gradually rose to my feet and walked to the kitchen to get some water. It was a very long journey. I was shaking and had to stop twice on the way to sit down because I was so weak. However, I *was* alive.

Drinking my water, I reflected on what could have happened a few minutes before. This was a wake up call, and I'd been given another chance. I decided, at that moment, to change my life, no matter how difficult it would be…

What I *didn't* know, until much later, was that in making this decision, I was taking my first step toward Godtown, and there would be no turning back. The journey had truly begun…

MY SECOND CHANCE

I know claiming that there was a voice in my head that talked to me seems extreme. I imagine you might be thinking, "Whoa, this chick is schizophrenic." Well, that's understandable, but please have patience and continue on with me because it's really important. I'd been wondering the same thing around this time, but couldn't deny that it had saved my life!

I was so shaken after my "heart attack," I had to pay attention and be a little open. I decided to trust I wasn't demon possessed and really communicate with it and see what would happen. This was a major step for me because trust was *not* one of my attributes, but figured I'd been given a second chance for a reason. Maybe this voice was supposed to be involved somehow. So I started spending time talking to it again and actually carried the *Godtown Guideline Handbook* with me wherever I went.

At first, it was kind of awkward because my friends, who were as much a part of Humanville as I'd been, didn't understand why I was acting so strange. They wanted to know what the book was. I told them it was something I'd found in a bookstore that had caught my eye. I didn't want to tell them about anything concerning my near death experience or the voice (and they knew nothing about my nightmare with eating disorders.) At the same time, I wasn't willing to leave the book at home. For some reason, I felt safe when carrying it and continually read from it. I would go back over the words, and they'd give me comfort.

They took up the hobby of teasing me and I put up with them because I wasn't ready to tell the truth. I didn't want to lie, but until it was all figured out, I just didn't feel right about being open with any of this. I was still concerned with what they thought and didn't want to appear to be a "kook," but slowly found myself leaving early from evenings out and even refusing invitations. I wasn't enjoying the "poor me" conversations anymore, and was just not interested in the scene. I started to prefer my own company to that of negative people with negative energy.

What a change for me! I was the *queen* of drama. I fed off of it! So, to recognize this and not want to enter into it was amazing. Something was happening, all right, and it was exciting. I continued to be open to the voice and began asking some real questions about life and issues that had confused me. The answers given were always fair, objective, unbiased, and love-based. Many times, they weren't answers I would've supported in the past, but I couldn't argue with logic based on love. I think it all started to make an impact on me because something interesting began to happen.

As I'd go through my normal day, people would react differently toward me. It was puzzling at first, because I didn't think I was doing anything different, but saw subtle changes and wondered what was causing them.

For instance, I went to my agent to check on any upcoming jobs. (I was still modeling on the side, occasionally, to pick up extra money. Hated doing it, but it was pretty mindless work. I battled body image constantly, but the "fear" I felt came across to the camera as *mystery*, I guess...go figure!) I noticed she had a peculiar look on her face. At first, it appeared negative, but then she smiled a little and seemed to relax. It was surprising because she was usually very stiff and curt, and I just thought she didn't like me. She actually said it had been good to see me and to "hurry back" as I was leaving. What was that all about? I went to my hairdresser. Same thing. What was going on? It happened over and over again.

Upon returning home later that day, I decided to have one of my little "talks" with the voice to find out. I sat down and cleared my mind and asked it to answer me. This was so cool because it said, "Yes, I am here for you, always. Whenever you ask me to come to you, I am already waiting."

Me: Well, umm, that's really great! Ok, I was wondering about something. I'm noticing people are reacting a little differently around me, and even though I like it...why?

Voice: It is your energy. You have been, up to this point, very guarded and protective. You did not come across as sincere. Now, you are slowly opening your heart because you are starting to trust that you can feel and show love. People are feeling this and reacting to it. You are just beginning to see the reflection of love...your love.

Me: Really? Wow, that's cool!. You mean, I'm creating this change?

Voice: Yes.

Me: But, I don't feel like I'm doing anything differently. How is this happening?

Voice: This is how love works. This is how I work. You don't have to *do* anything different, you are just *being* something different. You are light, not dark. It is really easy, isn't it? You didn't even know you were being light, did you?

Me: No, I didn't. I'm just attempting to be open to you and trying to trust I'm not crazy here. I still don't know what this is or who you are, but I must admit I'm starting to feel better inside, and that's a good feeling.

Voice: Oh, but you *do* know who I am, and what this is. You have always known. You just forgot as you were growing up in a very negative community. Every human comes into this world completely connected to love and to me.

At that moment, I stopped the conversation, suddenly knowing that, up until then, a very important question had not been addressed. I hadn't asked it yet because I was afraid. Yes…was scared to find out the answer. I could stall no more. It was too important to let it slip by again. I gathered my courage…

Me: I have to ask you something that I absolutely need to know. You say that every human is completely connected to you when they come into the world. I know you are the voice of love, but there's more to it than that…who are you?

Voice: Ahh, Desmond, I was hoping you would find the courage to ask me that question. I am very excited you overcame your fear and trust that you are ready to hear this answer. You are right, there is more to it, and also, there is no more to it. Does that sound confusing? Well, let me clarify. I *am* the voice of love. I am also God.

Me: You're kidding me, right? No way, you're God?

Voice: Yes, I am God. I am also love.

Me: Oh, my god!…umm, I mean…I kind of had a feeling that's the answer you'd tell me if I asked, but now that you've said it, I'm unsettled. It seems a little far-fetched that God could be inside of me and could be heard so clearly.

Voice: Trust I have always been with you, and that you have never been without love.

Me: You keep saying that, but it's a struggle. I haven't heard you before now…I would know!

Voice: As I told you just a moment ago, you could hear me when you were very young. You have forgotten because fear took over your heart, and you allowed it to control your life.

Me: I am trying to trust you and stay open to your words and guidance. It's just, I'm worried about my sanity. This seems very bizarre to me. I don't know how to believe you are really God!

Voice: Desmond, you are so afraid. You have been for so long, you cannot differentiate yourself from your fear. The pure heart you possess is covered with layers and layers of this negativity. It prevents you from trusting yourself. Become aware of your own power and your ability to shed all of those dark layers. Rejoice in the knowledge you are reconnecting with Me now, and remember how love feels. You are worthy of complete love.

I wanted to believe I was worthy. I wanted to believe this voice was God. I wanted to let go of my fear. The problem was, my lifetime had been spent listening to another voice that was the exact opposite of what I was now experiencing…

You see, for someone who has eating disorders, there's a constant war going on in our thought process. Some psychologists refer to this as the "negative mind." We create this "negative mind" ourselves by giving power to negative conditioning. I was very aware of my "negative mind" because it had convinced me of my unworthiness. What I didn't understand, until the voice of love entered my life, was what this "negative mind" was and where it came from.

As a child, a playmate made fun of my hair or a teacher said I talked too much during class. Maybe a parent disciplined me for going outside when I should've been studying, or an aunt made a passing statement about how I wasn't as cute as my sister. Who knows, for sure, what was said or who said what. The point is, in most cases, comments were made like this: "You look stupid. Your hair looks like a scarecrow." "Desmond! Shut-up! You're talking during class. You're a bad little girl and you have to be punished." "What? You went outside when I told you not too? You did that just to defy me. How dare you do that to me? You are an ungrateful, selfish child and you have to be punished." "Well, it's hard to believe you and your sister are from the same family. She's such a beauty!"

Do you understand what happened? Most of those comments were made flippantly, without a concern to how they were presented. I didn't know that they were born out of insecurity on the part of the presenter. The only things I heard were "stupid, bad, selfish, ungrateful, and ugly." I believed every word because I didn't receive enough support from the other side to counteract the influence these words had.

Maybe I was just oversensitive as a kid, but most people, if they were honest with themselves, would admit that negative words from those they cared about *did* have an effect on them. I didn't hear much positive reinforcement, so the negative won out. It's so vitally important to recognize that we all need encouragement and support.

The "negative mind" was the part of me that believed the negative comments I heard as a child. A deep insecurity developed inside me, and I took it to the extreme in order to please the very people who were hurting me. This was my way of trying to get approval. It was like, "See? I agree with you! I *am* a terrible person, like you said. In fact, look at me punishing myself. I respect your opinion. See how much I want your acceptance? I listen to what you say."

I finally understand that *other* people's fear created those negative comments. I wasn't a bad person. Unfortunately, I couldn't see this truth when I was young.

As I write to you now, I want to express that I do recognize the difference between the experience of love I was having with the voice of God and the "negative mind" voice *I'd* created because of my lack of self-worth. This is important to acknowledge because at that particular time, it was the basis of all of my struggles. I was forcing myself to consciously be open to the voice of love because it was second nature to allow my "negative mind" to dictate my life.

It really was a battle. The more I listened to my newfound voice, the harder it was to accept that I'd been so lost. I mean, my life hadn't been *that* screwed up, had it? Ok, yeah, it had been, but I wasn't ready to admit it yet…and I wasn't ready to give up my security blanket—my way of doing things. In other words, I wasn't ready to give up control of my life! At least that's what I thought the voice was telling me I had to do in order to be happy.

Slowly, though, a shift did start to occur. I kept having these conversations, and even through my defensive nature, some of the words started sinking in. I was seeing a change, both in my own life and in the lives of those around me. I vacillated and was still dealing with my eating disorder, but noticed I didn't turn to it *every* time I felt scared or hurt. On occasion, I'd seek the voice and meditate until the pain passed. It was rare, but it would always work. I'd either bury the pain then purge it, or stop and listen, letting the voice talk me through the problem. It would tell me that I was loved, and was worthy enough to let go of the problem without hurting myself.

I gotta tell you, I started to believe this voice might really be God. It felt a little strange because I knew others wouldn't understand—but I was just afraid of judgement. For the first time in many years, I wasn't turning to bulimia *every* time someone or something hurt me. And, you know, I was so thankful, it started not to matter what others might think of me or the voice. I was feeling hope and had not found it anywhere else.

I decided to hold on to my newfound relationship with the voice. I also decided to be open to the idea this *might* be God talking to me and trying to help me. I'd attempt not to let other's judgement interfere with that concept. I needed help, so why couldn't this be God? I mean, I was aware of miracles, and maybe this was one. Why not? It could happen, couldn't it?…

LIFE TAKES A TURN

I started taking one day at a time. I'd lost my publishing deal and my boyfriend had broken up with me, so this was a transition period. Usually, these make me crazy because I'm scared to death about money, the future, etc. This time wasn't as frightening. I mean, I did feel a little lost because I was trying to deal with life differently, and didn't know what the outcome would be. My desire, though, was to focus on love first, instead of getting angry or frustrated when things were tough. I'd feel peaceful every time I did, but the challenge was going there. I forgot to quite often.

The voice would always let me know, when I asked it, if my attempt to handle something was less loving than it could've been. For instance, I was on a fundraising committee for a very famous charity. There was another woman on it who was incredibly controlling and bossy. She'd take over meetings, dismiss any idea that wasn't hers, and try to assign the boring tasks to others while grabbing the "attention-getting" roles for herself.

One day, she tried to give me an awful job that would require hours and hours of phone and paperwork, and I told her I couldn't do it. There was too much on my mind (getting my career back on track, etc.) to be bothered with such a menial, low profile job. She started giving me the "guilt trip" speech, so I immediately got defensive and shut her down with some brilliant strategy I came up with in a pinch. (When in debate mode, I'd make any lawyer proud!) I pointed out that I'd already done my phone duty and could not recall the last time she'd served the charity in this manner. I also made her aware that we all had noticed she hadn't been present at the beginning of the last event, and had only shown up at the precise moment the media arrived. She strategically placed herself in camera view, finagled an interview, and then left the second the coverage was over. I then stated I was speaking for the entire group in saying that we were carrying the load for her, and made it clear everyone was tired of it.

Well, when you make a statement like that, you should be certain the people you're speaking for really back you up. Nobody did, in this situation. We'd all talked about how frustrated we were with her, but when the moment of truth came, no one else wanted to make waves. I was on my own! I was the one who ended up looking like the attention grabber and "crybaby". It was pretty humiliating. Needless to say, I left that meeting feeling awful. On the way home, I decided to run the situation by my inner voice to see what had happened.

Me: Ok, I obviously made an error in judgement back there, but she attacked me and I felt the need to stand up for myself!

Voice: Desmond, was this woman really attacking you? Or, was she trying to persuade you, in what she thought was an effective way, to serve the charity and do something that needed to be done?

Me: Well, when I told her I couldn't do the job, she got a very demeaning attitude and tried to make me feel horrible for saying no. She wasn't respecting my situation—or, well, I guess it was an excuse, really—and I resented it.

Voice: Think about it. Was she disrespecting you, or were you over-sensitive to the idea you really *do* have time to do this task because you are not working as much at present? Could it be you are upset and feel worthless over your professional situation and are overcompensating by acting too "busy" and "important" to fulfill this task? I suggest you realize that the purpose of this charity is to help very ill children. If you cannot honor the opportunity to help these children, then you should not be on this committee.

Me: Well, ok, you're probably right about being over-sensitive, but I'm sorry, there's not one person on that committee who's doing it only to help the children. This is a very high profile charity, and everyone wants to gain attention and get to interact with celebrities and power players, etc. I'm not unique in motivation, here!

Voice: Your actions should have nothing to do with another's motivations. If you are not pure in heart, you should not serve. It is as simple as that. No matter what this woman asks you to do, you need to graciously accept the task if you have volunteered to serve.

Me: So you're saying even when someone is being unfair to me, I should just do what she or he wants me to do? What about preserving my self-respect? You've told me to love myself, and I'm trying to do that! If someone's taking advantage of me, I must take a stand to defend my position!

Voice: Yes, I have told you to embrace and love your body, soul, spirit, and light. When you truly do this, you will understand that in a love-based existence, there is no need to defend your actions.

Me: Ok, you've lost me there. I don't have a clue what you are talking about.

Voice: Yes, I am aware of this. Desmond, why did you decide to join this committee? By the way, I already know the truth...

Me: Oh, all right, I know, I know. I joined to get media attention, and network with powerful people.

Voice: Did you think about what serving on this committee would entail?

Me: Well, I thought I'd go to functions, and, I don't know, walk around and talk to people about it, I guess…didn't put much thought into it, did I?

Voice: No, you didn't. You see, you were motivated by a fear-based need to feel important and recognized. This is an aspect of your insecurity. If you had volunteered to serve because you possessed a genuine love for those ailing children, your thoughts would be coming from an entirely different place…from love. You would be happy to do whatever was needed to help the children. Your attitude would be different. What's to defend when your desire is to be of service?

Me: Ok, yes, I do understand what you're saying, but I'm still confused about showing love for myself. I mean, here's a woman who's really controlling and bossing me around. It doesn't feel right.

Voice: If your heart is pure, and your motivation is loved-based, it is very easy to recognize the same spirit in others, and also the lack of spirit. This woman, let's assume her motivations are as self-indulgent as yours were, is also focusing on her insecurities and not love. If you are looking through loving eyes, you see her fear immediately, and do not personalize anything she says or does. Her actions are not about you, they are about her own lack of self-worth. Trust that it is extremely easy to see fear in others when you are not blinded by the same fear. Does this make sense?

Me: You know, it does. If I'm acting out of love, then there's no reason to take offense to someone else's fears. If this woman feels a void inside she's trying to fill by being "in charge," it's easy to see her motivation for being bossy. She's acting out of fear, and it has nothing to do with me. It's her issue, and I can choose how to respond to her. I possess the power to do so. I can love, or defend my own fear.

Voice: Very good, Desmond! You are beginning to understand. Very good.

So, there you have it…this was the start of my newfound approach to life, but, believe me, it was only the *very* start. As you will see, I had a long way to go…

SISTERHOOD

I mentioned I'd started carrying the *Godtown Guideline Handbook* around with me. I think you also know that my friends didn't understand what it was or why I was attached to it. Since this was the very beginning of my "journey" (I don't know how else to describe this experience…can't come up with anything more original. Please indulge my lack of creativity. I'll keep thinking about it…maybe something brilliant will hit me before too long!), I was tight-lipped around them. I was trying to fit in and be the person they all knew, but *was* changing and didn't want to hide the person I was starting to become.

We all attended an annual luncheon the week after my disastrous fundraising committee meeting. This was an event we went to every year and usually always enjoyed. It was held at a beautiful hotel in the heart of Humanville.

In the past, we'd all sit at the same table, start with cocktails and appetizers, work our way into wine and salad, swim our way into more wine and entrees, and dive our way into desserts and coffee, with Bailey's Irish Creme. By the time the program started, we'd usually be completely wasted, and the fun part of the day was trying to keep our composure while the speaker was talking. This, for us, meant trying not to slip off our chairs and slide under the table. Please don't misunderstand, we weren't the only table faced with this challenge. It was somewhat tradition with this particular event to kind of "let go," so most of the room would be pretty sloshed right along with us.

I was one of the last ones to arrive. I'd procrastinated, and almost didn't go, but then decided not to be a stick-in–the-mud. I sat by my friend Julie, who I'd known for many years but hadn't seen in a very long time. We'd met on a gig and realized we'd grown up near each other in the same suburb of Humanville. We were very different people, but shared common ground because of our upbringing. She'd been very successful as a singer, but unfortunately had recently gone through a divorce, so hadn't been hanging out with us for months.

Before we started indulging in food and drink, Julie turned to me and asked how I was doing. I said, "great," then before I could stop myself, corrected my statement and said that actually it was the best I'd ever been in some ways, and the most unsettled I'd ever been in some ways. Uh-oh, I'd just committed the ultimate faux pas in Humanville…I'd admitted vulnerability! Julie's face registered shock, but fortunately, before she said anything, a waiter interrupted us to take our orders.

I didn't want to have to explain, so turned to the friend on my left, Angela, and started a frivolous conversation with her about her favorite subject...her kid. All it took was one question, "How is Kennedy?" and off she went. I knew this would be an effective distraction from Julie's conversation because once Angela started in on "little Kenny," nothing could interrupt her. (I had to go to desperate measures to avoid continuing the other conversation.)

I just couldn't talk to anyone about any of this yet. I hoped Julie would forget by the time Angela finished, and as suspected, Angela didn't shut-up until dessert was served. The only upside to this excruciating conversation was the fact I didn't eat or drink very much. I was too busy looking at the latest pictures of "little Kenny" on a horse, "little Kenny" at the beach, "little Kenny" with his dog, etc.

(Oh...need to mention our table only lost one occupant to the floor this year. Rhonda kept up tradition in fine form and managed to slide off her chair with drink in hand, not spilling a drop! Never seen that done before... it was impressive!)

Anyway, after the luncheon, I was getting up to leave, and Julie took my arm and asked if I was in a hurry. She wanted to talk to me about something. (Damn, thought she'd forgotten!) I said I was actually kind of late for another appointment, but she told me it would only take a second. I said ok, so we gathered our things and went next door to a coffee shop.

After we found a table and sat down, she looked me in the eyes and asked, "What did you mean when you said this was the most unsettling time in your life?"

I stammered for a minute, not knowing how to answer. You see, these conversations are just not conducted in Humanville. One does not, under any circumstances, show vulnerability or weakness. It's not done. So, I was faced with a dilemma. Did I step out on my fragile new foundation and be honest, or go to my old safety net of fear and wiggle my way out of this? I bounced back and forth, yes-no, yes-no, until finally I closed my eyes, remembered "the heart attack," and realized it was time to be honest. I owed it to the voice. It had saved my life, and I *did* believe I was experiencing God.

I mustered up my courage, opened my eyes, looked at Julie, and said, "Well, funny you should ask me that," then proceeded to give her the cliff note version of my experience (minus the part about my eating disorders). The story had holes in it because I wasn't completely candid, but was thorough enough to make sense. After I finished, I fully expected her to get up and leave, run from this "crazy" woman, but she didn't. She just sat there for a minute, then said very softly, "Thank you for telling me your experience. I've had the same thing happen to me, but haven't told anybody about it."

I nearly jumped out of my chair! I grabbed her arm and practically yelled, "You have a voice? You hear God? You know what I'm talking about?"

She said, "Yes, I think I do."

I was ecstatic, and asked her to please tell me about it! She proceeded to share her story with me. It was similar, but there were differences. She'd lost a brother to death after her divorce and had been very angry at the world. She was bitter and almost destroyed her own life because of her grief and was literally on her knees with despair. When she was at the deciding moment—would she or wouldn't she end it all—a strange thing happened. A window suddenly blew open and a strong breeze swept into her bedroom where she was kneeling. Even though it was cold outside, this wind was very warm, almost balmy. It blew with a force, but felt gentle as it wrapped itself around and embraced her. Then it lifted her into a standing position. Julie thought she was going out of her mind, but at the same time, she also felt safe and protected. As quickly as it had entered, the wind blew out of her room. She was left shaken, but standing. When she walked over to shut the window, there was a young woman standing on her lawn. She quickly ran downstairs and opened the front door. The thought didn't occur to her to be afraid of the stranger, although normally she would've been. She stepped out on her front porch and looked around, but the woman was nowhere to be found. Julie then ran out into her yard and peered down the street, but still, no one was there. As she turned to go back into her house, she noticed something lying on her front steps. She'd been in such a hurry, she'd stepped over it. It looked like a book. She picked it up. The cover said "The Godtown Guideline Handbook." She opened it and saw one word... "listen."

I jumped out of my chair and almost screamed! I caught myself and just laughed out loud. She grabbed my hand and pulled me back down to my chair.

"Desmond, it was so confusing. I mean, I didn't know what all this was about. I thought I was hallucinating, but there was the handbook thing, and it was real. I could feel it in my hands! I threw myself on the floor and started to cry. That's when I first heard a voice in my mind calling to me and comforting me. I wasn't afraid, for some reason, just unsettled by the experience."

I said, "Yeah, I know!!! The same thing happened to me! Let me show you." I reached into my purse and pulled out my handbook. She gasped, then reached out and touched the book. She didn't take it from me.

"I carry this with me everywhere I go now. It gives me comfort." I explained.

Julie didn't say anything, but I could tell she was relieved that my handbook was with me and it was, in fact, a tangible object. I wanted to hear more about her experience, so asked, "Did you respond to the voice?"

She replied, "Well, at first, I didn't know what to do, but continued to listen to what it was whispering to me. It told me it loved me, and that I was not finished serving my purpose. My time to leave the planet was not at hand. I finally responded and asked what it was. The voice said the same thing it said to you, that this was the voice of love and was also God. I asked why God was all of a sudden contacting me, and the whisper answered that I was the one who was reaching out. It said I was finally at a point where I had no place to turn and was forced to acknowledge love's presence. It also added that I'd been living in fear for most of my life."

I was overjoyed to hear Julie say these things. I empathized with her
confusion, but was excited about the fact she was opening her life up to a
possible "miracle" also. I told her so. She smiled at me and agreed that she
felt she'd been given a miracle. She then said the voice told her that her
brother was still in her life and lived on in her heart. It also let her know he
had fulfilled his purpose on this plane, and had gone to the next one. She
asked if I understood what that meant. I told her I had no idea, and
suggested she ask the voice about it. She wasn't sure she'd be comfortable
doing that. I understood, but gave her an assurance that conversing with her
"voice" would not be a bad experience. Quite the contrary, it would be very
enlightening if she could find the courage to do so. (I had to laugh at myself
because I was sounding like such an elder statesman, but in truth, was
almost as clueless as she was about all this. I was just a little ahead of her
in the "let's keep an open mind" area, that's all.) She seemed grateful for
this advice. I also asked if she'd looked in her handbook again since that
first time, and she shook her head "no." I told her open it when she got
home. She'd be amazed at what was now in it. That didn't make much
sense to her, but she stated she'd do so, anyway.

Julie then asked about Godtown. I told her I wasn't sure what or where it
was yet, but did believe there was a Godtown and that it was possible to live
there, someday. I just hadn't been able to figure out how or when that would
happen. She asked if I'd continued to interact with my "voice," and I told
her that it had become a big part of my life. I admitted I'd had the same
hesitations she was having, especially in the beginning, but was slowly
overcoming them. I also stated that I thought she'd been braver than I
because she'd asked and had been open enough to hear that the voice of love

was also God. It had taken quite a while for me to muster up the courage to ask that question. She smiled, responding that she was feeling anything but courageous, but appreciated my vote of confidence.

We ended our conversation by agreeing to keep in touch with each other. Upon leaving, Julie turned to me and asked, "Desmond, do you really believe these inner voices of ours could be God?" I paused for a moment, then answered, "I'm beginning to think that maybe it's a definite possibility. How's that for an ambiguous answer?" She laughed and said, "You've missed your calling. Politics is beckoning you!" I told her I'd consider it if the music thing fell through. She laughed again, then said bye. I knew we'd be talking again very soon...

THIS ONE'S DIFFICULT...

I walked to my car in deep thought. Julie had gone through almost the same experience as I had. She'd heard her inner voice during her most desperate hour, just like me. I found that interesting and reassuring, actually. Since two of us were going through this, it was validating.

I drove home thinking about Julie's loss. I'd never met her brother, but she talked about him all the time. He was young—mid thirties—married, and had two children. She'd idolized him. While being a professor of psychology at a prestigious university, he'd written two books on child rearing, one of which had landed on the bestseller list providing him with an element of celebrity. He developed a rare form of cancer and fought it for three years before finally losing the battle. I knew he'd been sick but thought he was in remission. Julie also thought he'd conquered it, but apparently the disease had flared up again quickly and took his life within a matter of weeks.

I was very confused about disease, injury, and death. It was so hard to understand how any of these experiences could be looked upon in a positive light. My voice was telling me that everything had the potential to be viewed through love. I just didn't buy that death, injury, or disease had much, if anything, to do with love. To me, they all seemed like unnecessary suffering. So, I decided to have a little chat with "God" during my drive home.

Me: Ok, I don't get the concept of death being a part of love. I think death is a horrible thing, especially in a situation where a young person or a child is taken early. It doesn't seem fair.

Voice (God): Desmond, when someone dies, you interpret it from a human viewpoint. It makes no sense to you that an innocent child or a young adult could be taken. How could this happen? How could this person be robbed of his or her life? You become angry, just as Julie did. What you need to understand is that every person has lessons to be learned and love to spread. You have no idea how many hearts one soul can touch as he or she goes through life. My logic and timing make no sense to you because the world says a long life is best. That is not necessarily true. When someone you care about leaves you, there is a void in your heart. You miss this person, and grieve for *your* loss. You see, every human comes into the world with a unique purpose. If you understood that death is actually rebirth, you would not be afraid of it. You would be happy for any human who had fulfilled his or her purpose, and would rejoice when that person had the blessing of rebirth. You would still miss your loved one, for this is how your heart holds onto the soul. You have to trust I know and love all living beings and operate on My time schedule, not one you think is right. Since death is an unknown to you, you fear it, and your fear interprets death as negative. I am telling you rebirth is glorious, a wonderful part of life.

Me: Ok, God, I really want to believe you right now, but considering how much a person can suffer during the dying process or when injured, I just can't accept that this is a part of love.

Voice (God): Yes, fear does manifest itself into suffering. Do you understand you have the power to choose how to interpret any situation you go through? If you believe that physical pain or sickness cannot be approached and dealt with through love, then you become vulnerable to it. You give it power over you, and it does become a horrible experience. However, realizing you have the ability to love *through* the experience of sickness and physical pain helps you not succumb to weakness. Even when faced with a serious injury or disease, you can choose to deal with it either using love or fear. Love will open your heart up to see all the blessings that can come out of these situations. I know you may not understand this, but many miracles can occur during the process of dealing with injury and disease. The opportunity to trust your faith in Me, to find your true strengths based on love, and to see how others bestow love to you will be awe-inspiring. When approaching these situations in a positive way, your energy alone will help the healing process because it will be light, not dark. If you choose to deal with the situation through fear, it will be a nightmare and you will feel overwhelmed, angry, and scared. Your heart will be in a dark place, and yes, it will be challenging to heal in this case. When humans become ill or injured, they are in a humble state of being because, basically, they fear they have no control. As long as fear is in command, they create more dis-ease, causing a response that does not allow love to flow. When positive energy is given the opportunity to flourish, miracles can happen. In other words, the power of love is strong enough to ease your suffering during sickness or pain. It can also heal the body and the mind.

Me: Ok, now this is getting freaky. Are you telling me that I have the power to heal my own body and overcome even fatal disease? If that's the case, why are there medical professions, drugs, doctors, heart transplants and things like that? I don't get it.

Voice: I will tell you the physical body has a tremendous amount of healing power that most beings don't realize or understand. Fear is so associated with disease that in many cases, love is not even given the opportunity to heal. I have given the gift of medical science to help guide and aid in the healing process. It is a tremendous part of love. I have also bestowed the gift of spiritual healing to some. The two types of healers can work hand in hand. They are all a part of the power of love and positive healing.

Me: Well, what about when none of it works? When medicine fails, and spiritual healing fails, and the body can't heal itself. Then death results!

Voice (God): As I have already explained, death is actually rebirth and should not be feared. When a human has completed his or her purpose on the planet, then rebirth occurs. Trust that I live in the heart of every being. I love and guide every soul through this transition. I recognize there is much fear when dealing with sickness, pain, or dying. If you can perceive everything through the eyes of love, you can see the opportunity to trust your faith, love, and Me in every situation. It is a part of life. You possess so much power and strength! You are a part of the entire universe, and are connected to everything and everyone because I am in and a part of everything and everyone. Are you beginning to understand who I am and how everything potentially has the opportunity to flow together through love?

Me: Yeah, I guess so. It's a little overwhelming, to be honest, but I made a commitment to be open to you and these conversations so I won't dismiss anything you just told me. It's just a struggle believing all of it. To hear you say that we don't die until our purpose has been fulfilled is reassuring, but I've never thought like this before. I've been afraid of death, and have also experienced pain before, so it's frightening. I don't know, the whole concept of God being so real and personal is new and foreign to me. I mean, before I discovered you I didn't believe in God, really. I thought maybe you were around, sort of, but I certainly didn't think God could be so here for me. God was a very esoteric concept, so please be patient with me. Maybe in time I'll settle into this and feel comfortable. I *do* want to trust your words concerning disease, injury, and death.

Voice (God): Desmond, I always have been, and always will be, patient with you. I will never leave you and will always be available to you at any moment in time. I am very happy you finally asked for Me to be an active part of your life. Also, I acknowledge the courage you showed with Julie by telling her about your experience. You are beginning to overcome fear. This is a very good thing.

Me: Why, thank you. I guess you're giving me a star for the day, huh?

Voice (God): Yes, you just have to realize you can "get a star" *every* day if you choose love. *Every* day...

I actually had been home for about ten minutes but was still in my car. My neighbor came outside at one point and just stared at me because he thought something was wrong. I was just sitting there, gazing straight ahead. You know, I don't even know what it must look like when I "talk to God" because I don't close my eyes or anything. Just have to clear my mind and get out of my own way to hear the voice. Is this weird to you? Or do you kind of understand what I'm talking about? You don't have to answer that question, I'm just pondering for a second...Ok, onward...

THAT'S *MY* MANAGER!

A few days after the luncheon, I woke up in a panic (after I'd had a bad dream...fear again) realizing I had to get my professional life back on track. I wasn't generating much income, other than the occasional modeling jobs, and had somewhat dropped the ball on my music focus. Being so wrapped up in my new spiritual journey thing, I'd kept "real" life on the back burner.

I got up quickly and made coffee, and paced the floor while drinking my first cup, frantically thinking about where to begin. I started to get angry with myself for letting my career slide and was almost in tears when something dawned on me. I'd gone to my inner voice for guidance about personal things, so why not ask for assistance in my professional life? It seemed strangely uncomfortable asking for help in this area because, the truth is, I didn't feel deserving when it came to my career. Asking seemed selfish when it had to do with anything concerning professional success.

I decided to not bother the voice with this dilemma. I could do it on my own. My first task was to sit down and make a phone call to the manager I'd been working with and to a few other connections I had. When finished, I showered and dressed, then hit the street.

First, I went to my modeling agency to check on any upcoming jobs. They had nothing for me, so I just let them know of my availability. The next stop was the musician's union to put up one of my "background singer" flyers on the bulletin board. I hadn't done that in ages, thinking I was way beyond having to use a flyer for gigs, but was desperate and needed work. Then I called a friend, who worked with me periodically, and asked if he could go to lunch. Luckily, he wasn't booked, and agreed to meet me at a favorite lunch spot in the city.

I couldn't wait to see him because he was one of those people who always made me laugh. His name was Jimmy and he was one of the best studio guitarists and background vocalists in the industry. We'd worked on a number of projects together and I felt somewhat close to him. It was purely a professional friendship. Even though I'd always thought he was really cute, it wasn't an option because I was into a sleek image when it came to men. Jimmy was a little too "earthy" for me. (I can't believe I just admitted that to you, but by now I've pretty much bared my soul, so why not let you know about my shallow criteria for guys, too!?!) Looking back, Jimmy, I'm sure, suspected this about me and had never shown the slightest romantic interest. He was one of the few people I knew in the industry who seemed to have integrity. In truth, it was surprising he even cared for me at all, considering how fake my personality must have appeared to him. I was becoming aware of my public persona and was a little embarrassed thinking about it. I only knew how to deal with the industry in one way, so almost cursed the voice for taking my blinders off and letting me see how unbecoming many of my actions had been in the past. The thing was, I couldn't imagine trying to interact with most of these people in a pure, loving way. It just seemed too vulnerable, and the sharks—as I referred to the power players—would swallow me whole if I let them interact with the "new" me. Nonetheless, Jimmy did seem to like me, so I was looking forward to seeing him and picking his brain about work possibilities.

When I got to the restaurant, he was already at a table, waiting. I caught his eye, waved, then hurried over and sat down across from him. (He was such an attractive man! The most beautiful eyes I'd ever seen…always went through the same thought process when I'd see Jimmy. Ok, had to quit being distracted and get back to focus!!) We chit-chatted for a few minutes—and, as always, he made me laugh—then ordered our lunch.

When our food was served, he took a couple of bites and then eased into a conversation I was fully unprepared to have. He said, "Desmond, did I tell you I'm working with a new female artist who just got signed over at Ultimate Records?"

I answered, "No, Jimmy. I haven't seen you for a while. That's cool. How long have you been on the gig?"

Jimmy said, "Well, I got the call a few weeks ago from her manager, Lou Pasterelli."

I almost dropped my fork! Lou was *my* manager! What the hell was he doing working with *another* female artist!?! I couldn't hide my shock and almost choked on my food, so grabbed my water and took a big swallow before answering. I cleared my throat and then said as non-chalantly as possible, "Well, that must be exciting for you. Who's the artist?"

Jimmy answered, "Oh, you know her. It's Trinity Lyons. Remember, we all worked together on that TV special last year? She sang back up with you."

Of course I remembered! Trinity Lyons! I couldn't believe it! How could *she* get a record deal? And, more importantly, what was she doing working with *my* manager!?! I tried to keep my composure when replying, knowing I was about to explode with anger but not wanting to show that to Jimmy.

I said as sweetly as possible, "Wow, Jimmy, that's great. What are you doing with her?"

He said, "The label has hired me to be her musical director. She's in the studio now, and I'm playing and singing on the record, but then she'll tour as soon as the first single hits radio. Rumor has it the label's pouring more money into her than they ever have on a new artist. Supposedly, she's going to be their next big superstar. At least she should be, considering how much they're spending on her."

I was getting sick to my stomach. How could this be happening? Trinity and I fell into the same market. We had a similar style, and she even resembled me, a little—well, she had the same hair color, and was about the same build and body type—it's just, I was a much better singer! When we'd worked together the year before, I had to teach her harmony part to her and even give her the right pitch before every song. She had a terrible ear! To make matters worse, Ultimate Records was the best label in the industry. That was where I'd dreamed of being signed. In fact, Lou and I had talked about that very thing happening. Jimmy interrupted my thoughts by throwing the final blow.

He said, "Hey, we're looking for a back-up singer to tour with us. In fact, there'll be studio work available immediately, then the tour will start and last at least a year. We'll be two months on, one month off, at first. You interested?"

I just couldn't answer. Here I was, trying to get back on track and needing work, but not shadow work like this. I was *not* going to sing back-up for Trinity Lyons, no way!! I'd pull my fingernails out first! I graciously told Jimmy I'd check my book and see about availability, then get back to him. All I wanted to do was get out of there, and fortunately, he had a 2:00 meeting so he had to run, also. He picked up the check, which was kind, and told me to let him know as soon as possible. I smiled, said bye, and then literally ran to my car.

I barely got the door unlocked and behind the wheel before bursting out in tears. How could Lou do this to me? I mean, true, I hadn't talked to him in a few weeks, but he'd thrown money into my project and everything! We hadn't formally signed a contract yet, but we were working on a verbal agreement, I thought, and <u>he had spent money on me, damn it</u>! I hadn't done anything to upset him, surely. It wasn't my fault I couldn't get into the studio to finish my project. The engineer had been booked for a month and wasn't even available. I fully intended to contact him and book studio time for the next week but had wanted to talk to Lou first. That's why I'd put a call in to him earlier in the day. He hadn't returned it yet, but that wasn't unusual. I figured I'd hear from him by early evening…but, all of a sudden I wasn't sure if he would call me back, now.

At that moment, I made a hasty decision to drive over to Lou's office and talk to him, face to face. He had a lot of explaining to do! I tried to dry my eyes, fix my make-up, and gain my composure before starting the car. Finally thought I was together enough to drive, so I left the restaurant's parking lot and headed cross-town to the westside (where Lou's office was located.)

Humanville is so frustrating to drive in because the freeway system is totally over-saturated with cars, and the side roads are in terrible disrepair. Traffic is always backed up, and as a result, it took me over an hour and a half to reach Lou's office. By the time I got there, I was about to explode! My road rage did nothing to calm my anger at Lou, so needless to say, I walked into his reception area fuming. I yelled at the receptionist to tell Lou I needed to see him immediately! She replied he was on the phone, and I told her I'd wait until he got off, but was not leaving until I saw him.

She tried to be polite and asked me to sit down, but I said that I'd prefer to stand. I didn't move...just hovered over her desk so she wouldn't forget about me. I obviously was making her uncomfortable, but I didn't care. I was going to get to the bottom of this situation as quickly as possible, and was not going to be deterred by some receptionist who kept giving me dirty looks!

Thirty minutes passed by, but don't think for a second that I was waiting patiently. About every, oh I'd say minute and a half, I'd ask her again if Lou had finished his conversation. I was driving her crazy, but she was trying to be calm with me. I was purposely agitating her because I felt like it. I had to vent my anger somewhere!

Finally, she announced Lou was indeed off the phone. (Her look of relief was almost comical.) She buzzed him and announced I was in the lobby requesting to see him. I saw her hesitate, glance at me, and then quietly tell him I wouldn't leave. She said "yes sir," then looked at me as if I was heading to the gas chamber and told me to go back to Lou's office, for he would see me now. I smiled at her with a smirk, then marched back there with guns drawn, ready for battle. The second I walked through his door, I knew the war was over. Trinity's picture was plastered everywhere! Posters, promotional packages, a full-sized cardboard stand-up. You name it, Trinity's picture was on it.

I walked over to Lou's desk and just looked at him. He gave me a sleazy manager smile and said, "Desmond, great to see you! Have a seat."

He motioned to a chair across from his desk, and I sat down as told, feeling sick to my stomach. (Lou has those ridiculous "power chairs" I hate so much. You know the ones that sit across the desk from him and are about ten inches lower than his chair, so you feel like a little kid when you sit in them. They make you have to look up, and as much as I hate to admit it, they're effective, because I was feeling about seven years old at that moment.) Anyway, I started to say something, but he cut me off.

"Desmond, I'm glad you're here, because I was just about to call you back. There's something we need to talk about." (Yeah, I'd say so!) "I don't know if you've heard, but I'm representing Trinity Lyons now." (As if that wasn't obvious. He had a damn "Trinity" shrine in his office!) "I've just secured a recording contract for her with Ultimate Records," (yeah, yeah, yeah) "and I'm just swamped right now. She's in the studio, as we speak, and I'm in the middle of setting up her tour schedule and securing sponsorship for her. As a result, I'm going to have to let go of some of my other clients for the time being. I know we hadn't formally signed anything, and I'm kicking myself because I'm such a schmuk for not protecting my interest. I put quite a bit of money into your project and I can't get that back. You know, kid, I don't even care. You're a sharp one, getting me to do all that without paper, but, hey, you played the game better than I did. I admire that, so let's just call it even. How's that?"

What did he mean, "how's that"? What did he expect me to say!?! I wasn't "playing a game" with him. I hadn't been trying to outwit him, and he knew that. He was just bullshitting me because he knew the money he'd spent on me was chicken feed compared to what he had received with Trinity's contract. Good grief, just in signing commission alone he probably received twenty times what he'd spent on me. With endorsements, merchandising, royalties, etc., his 15% commission of Trinity's income would be worth a fortune if she hit. And according to Jimmy, there was a good chance she would with that much label support. Shit!!!

I looked at Lou and just said one word. I opened my mouth and asked, "Why?" His sleazy smile faded and, for one brief second, he let his guard down.

He said to me, "Hey, Trinity bugged the hell out of me, drove me crazy. She wouldn't leave me alone, taking me out, buying me shit, wining and dining me. She kept pestering me to listen to her stuff. I finally did and thought she had potential, so I started working with her. Even though she was green, I kept molding her and it paid off!"

At that moment, I knew the truth. I looked him straight in the eye, and said, "You're fucking her, aren't you?" He didn't reply, but just raised his hands up and shrugged his shoulders like, "Yeah, so what?"

I didn't respond…just got up and walked out the door…didn't look back… kept my eyes straight ahead until I got out of the building and to my car. The war was over, and I'd lost. Hadn't even been in the battle, really. If I had to sleep with Lou in order to get a record deal, then I wasn't in the game. I mean, I'm not stupid enough to think those things didn't happen, and I'd been hit on a number of times. It's just, I wanted to believe talent was more important than sleaze and that in the end the most gifted artist won. I should've known better than to believe that.

Once again, I found myself totally heartbroken. What was going on? What was I doing that was so terribly wrong it warranted this kind of disappointment? I couldn't get a break. Short of prostituting myself, how could this latest fiasco have been avoided? I drove home in a state of shock. This one really hurt. All of them did, actually, but I just couldn't believe it had happened again! I kept falling off the horse. Couldn't keep my balance, only this time the horse had run under a branch and knocked me off. It wasn't my fault!

I felt this overwhelming urge to bury the hurt. As usual, my focus shifted immediately from the painful experience to the "quick fix"... yes, bulimia. I started thinking about what was at home to accomplish the act. I did a quick mental inventory, then decided to stop at the store to stock up. Typical behavior. I'd been through this a million times before. I pulled into the parking lot of a quick stop and got out of the car.

I started to go in, but hesitated for a second because a thought entered my mind. I'd been at this crossroads many times in the last few weeks, and had, on occasion, turned to the voice for help. I could do that now. Oh, I didn't want to! I wanted the pain to go away quickly! Someone had to step around me to walk out of the store because I stood frozen, blocking the doorway. I was too busy trying to make a decision about what to do. (The voice never interjected in these decision-making thoughts. In fact, it never spoke up unless I asked it to. I believe this is what God refers to as my "free will." I had the ability to ask for guidance, or not. My choice was always honored.) Anyway, I finally made myself listen because, for some reason, I let down my blinders for a second. It must have been when the guy stepped around me. It broke my train of thought and a moment of clarity crept in...

I asked for help, saying I wanted to bury my pain, but knew I shouldn't do it—that everything was out of control. The voice responded, as usual, with love and wisdom.

Voice (God): Desmond, you want the pain to go away and know you can temporarily fix the hurt by practicing an act that will ultimately destroy you. In truth, you feel you deserve to be destroyed because you think what happened today was actually your fault. You felt worthless in the manager's office. This is something you always carry with you, and he confirmed it by rejecting you. You truly believe his opinion is so much more important than yours. You also think his actions are directly associated with you and that he is giving attention to the other singer to show how unworthy you are.

None of his actions has anything to do with you. I assure you he is not thinking about you at all. He is very lost in a tremendous fear he masks as arrogance. If you could crawl into his mind and understand his motivations, you would see he is very afraid.

Me: Lou, afraid? I find that hard to buy. That man is the epitome of confidence.

Voice (God): If Lou was confident, he would not feel like he had to buy affection. He is very insecure, and thinks that only in providing Trinity with something she wants will she give him attention in return. He is right. She has no real caring for him. She is being bribed and is bribing him in return. When a relationship is built on a selfish foundation, there is nothing to hold it together except self-absorbed motivation. There is no reaching out to each other and no love to bond with. Think about it, if they felt love-based desire for each other, they would absorb each other's hearts and spirits and would merge and become a strong pillar, which could weather even the most powerful storm. Self-absorbed motivation does not allow merging and, in fact, absorbs its own spirit, ultimately absorbing itself. Think of a black hole, if you know what that phenomenon is. It destroys itself by imploding. So it is with humans who operate out of self-absorbed desire. Do you understand what I am illustrating?

Me: I do, actually. It's wild, I don't even think of Lou as having real human emotions. He is so slick in business, I guess I can't imagine he has feelings and desires.

Voice (God): Every human has sincere longings and desires to feel love. The saddest aspect of this situation is the fact that both Lou and Trinity will ultimately have to deal with the consequences of their choices. Any action that is not motivated by love is motivated by fear. Fear always leads to a path of difficulty and suffering. Remember the discussion about disease and death? Fear manifests into suffering. You will see, in time, what I am referring to in this situation.

Me: Do you mean the relationship between Lou and Trinity will fall apart?

Voice (God): I am saying they both will have to be responsible for their choices. Nothing more needs to be said. Time will bring your answer. Now, there is something I need to tell you concerning your reaction to the news you heard today. You felt overwhelming jealousy and anger when you found out Trinity had been given a recording contract. You immediately went to a place of fear because, once again, you personalized the news and thought it was an attack on you. Your reaction was not loved-based in any way. Do you know why you reacted in such a negative way?

Me: Oh, God, I was so defeated and unfairly treated. I've worked just as hard as Trinity and am a better singer. She was given my dream, and I felt robbed.

God: Yes, you did. What if you had gone past those feelings and reacted through love? So many things would have turned out differently for you today. If you had asked Me for guidance before you even stepped outside your door this morning, I could have aided in your path and you would have had a joyous experience. Instead, you wanted to do it yourself. Desmond, I am always here for you, in all aspects of your life. You are worthy of love in everything you say, do, and are. You never have to feel selfish about asking for guidance. You have a purpose to fulfill, and I am here to help you achieve that goal.

In your discussion with Jimmy, if you had lovingly supported the news about Trinity's record deal, you would not have been blinded by jealousy. You would have recognized that there is plenty of opportunity for both of you, and giving of your talents does not require competition. When you use the gifts I have given you for service, and depend on divine guidance to help you serve, doors open easily. I am opening them. You just have to walk through. It is as simple as that. It only requires faith. This brings me to the next topic. Why do you want to acquire a record deal? For what reasons?

Me: Well, I want to share my music with the world, and...umm, ok, that's not necessarily true...I want to be famous. That's the real reason. I want to feel important and be treated with respect so I'll feel special.

God: Yes, I know this. Your motivations are not really about service. What drives you is not unlike what drives Trinity. Both of you have felt a lack of self-worth, and both have mistakenly assumed fame would bring you self-love.

Me: Yeah, well maybe so, but Trinity gets to find out and it's not looking like I'll ever have the chance to let people hear my songs.

God: There you go, putting yourself in a box. You can only see one way of getting to share your music. If you don't get a record deal, then you have failed and will never get to sing for the public. You are limiting yourself. I suggest you look outside your "box" for your fulfillment.

Me: What are you talking about?

God: I am saying that a record deal with Ultimate Records is only one, small avenue to reach the world. In fact, for you, it could easily be a very limiting road to go down. Look in other directions.

Me: What other directions?

God: If you trust Me and have faith that I will guide you, I will show you the way to go. It's time you realize that the key to fulfilling your purpose is through embracing and appreciating the process, the journey. You have never understood this concept. This brings me to the next issue I need to discuss with you. The process.

Me: Ok, what are you talking about? I know you want me to ask, so I'll bite. Go ahead.

God: Yes, I will, thank you. Desmond, your struggle with bulimia is, in part, a way for you to try to avoid the process of living. You have never appreciated the fact that in order to reach a goal, you have to go through a process, and this is really the important part of the goal. It is where all the beautiful lessons live and where love grows. Reaching the goal is just the end product of the journey. It is the journey itself that holds the real excitement and energy. You have been afraid of the process because you have feared you will fail if you really try to go through it. So you keep one foot out the door by focusing on bulimia. It is your out—your hiding place. You have not believed you could actually achieve success because of your lack of self-confidence. I am here to tell you that you *can* achieve success, and all you have to do is understand the joy you can feel in the process. It is so simple it is easy to miss.

Me: I guess so, because I've missed it my entire life!

God: That is not true. You knew this when you were very young. When you were still connected to Me and had not been influenced by the world around you.

Me: Wait a minute!! Oh my god!! Oops...I mean, I do remember this! Being like, three or so, and feeling totally together. Now I know why this experience with You has seemed so familiar! You were very present in my heart, soul, and spirit when I was a young child. I didn't know any better than to be open to You, and I didn't start to lose You until I listened and believed the words and actions of the people around me who said negative things. You've been reminding me, but I had too much fear until now. I remember!!

God: Yes. I have never left you.

Me: Wow, this is incredible! How did I lose You for so long?

God: You just misplaced Me, you never lost Me. No one ever can lose Me, but one can choose not to acknowledge Me. Often, it is a subconscious decision. I am under layers and layers of fear.

Me: All these years, all of this time, I could have turned to You...could I have avoided the nightmare of anorexia and bulimia if I'd understood that You were always with me?

God: Yes, you could have had experienced love in every moment of your life.

Me: I'm heartsick about turning away from You, but I was a child and didn't realize there was a choice, did I?

God: This is the unfortunate aspect of human fear. Your background is an example of what happens to children when the community around them is based on negative energy. You were raised in an environment where anything outside of the "bubble," as you call it, was construed as "bad." In other words, you developed a fear of the unknown. The interesting aspect of your upbringing is that your parents were actually carrying on with the fear they were raised in. The energy was passed from generation to generation. This does not mean your parents and grandparents were "wrong," they were just as blinded by fear as the generation before them. Also, the world around them was full of fear, and they were reacting to their environment.

Me: This is making sense to me, but why didn't You reach out to them as You are to me? I mean, didn't my parents and grandparents get to a point of desperation, too? Didn't they call out to You as I did?

God: Yes they did, every one of them. I was there, always, in each life, ready to serve their needs. Your parents, grandparents, and ancestors are all beautiful souls and I love them all with the same unconditional love in which I love you. You are very blessed to have a wonderful family.

Me: Well, thank you, I guess. It's just, if You were there to guide them, then why were they so afraid when they were raising me, and why were my grandparents afraid raising my parents, etc.? Why wasn't all of this pain avoided?

God: I am in every human heart, waiting to be a loving, guiding light in every life. However, each human must ask Me for guidance and be open to accept My love. Every human heart has it's own, unique timing. In your family's case, your relatives have asked for My guidance many times and have experienced My love. As you exemplified today, though, even with the knowledge I am here for you in every moment, you still chose not to turn to Me. You dealt with your life without My help. You did not want Me involved in your decisions. All humans have the free will to decide when I am present in their lives and when they want to shut Me out. So it was with your relatives. Sometimes each one of them turned to Me, and sometimes each tried to handle life without My love. Do you understand?

Me: Yes, I do. Why is it so hard to turn to You when we know that by doing so, our lives would be easier and less painful?

God: You answered this question a few minutes ago when you wanted to "bury your pain" through bulimia. Now that you have come to Me for help, you can see the truth behind the experience you had with your manager. You almost didn't ask Me for guidance. You have free will to decide what path to take in every decision and situation. Every human possesses free will. The option to choose love is always open to each of you, but there are times when you feel My guidance will take you away from something you want. If you come to Me, I might tell you "no," that the way you want to take is not the best, most loving direction you can go. Even though you understand that My guidance is always based on love and given to you for your ultimate happiness, you don't want to hear My words. So you choose the direction you want to go. Remember, every decision in life is based either on love or fear. Since I am complete unconditional love and My words express this love, you choose another path, which is fear. As a result, your choice will lead to painful consequences. Fear always results in disappointment, pain, frustration, anger, injury, etc. It is inevitable.

It is very important to understand that these consequences are not punishment from Me. I do not punish. I heal, I forgive, I am love. I am deeply saddened when you turn away from love and from Me because I am still with you, watching your struggle, feeling your pain, and desiring you to reach for Me. The very essence of love is gentle, kind, non-judgmental, and non-aggressive...this is the ultimate power of love. So, as much as I want to help, I love you enough to wait patiently for you to go through the process of consequence. Lessons will be learned and you will grow to understand that love is the only path to true happiness and joy.

To specify what I am explaining, I will address the struggle you face with bulimia. You have chosen to bury your light in this disease because you have decided you are not worthy of your own love. Let me ask you, do you love Me?

Me: Well, yes, God. I acknowledge my gratitude for Your guidance and want you to know how much You mean to me. I've never felt so safe and loved, and I'm starting to have brief moments of true joy. That is, when I really allow myself to believe You are real and trust what you tell me. So, yes, I do love You.

God: Do you believe I am a part of you?

Me: Well, obviously. I mean, I'm having conversations with You inside my mind, so I have to believe You're a part of me to feel comfortable about these interactions. If I didn't, I'd think I was completely nuts!

God: Desmond, I assure you that you are not "nuts." You are, however, rejecting Me every time you hurt your body by practicing bulimia. If you love Me, then you must love yourself, because I am a part of you and you are a part of Me. If you punish your body, you are punishing Me. I will still love you unconditionally and so will your body. Think about it. How many times have you punished and rejected your body by starving or bingeing and purging? Countless times, right? Do you realize that your body loves you so much that it has suffered and taken your abuse and still performed for you? It has continued to try to move, pump blood, sleep, and do all the bodily functions it is supposed to do, even though you are torturing it every chance you get. It loves you that much. I love you that much. We are one, and when you finally realize how unbelievably beautiful you are in My eyes and love yourself as you do Me, you will heal from your disease because you will finally love your body and desire to honor it. You will see that the body, the spirit, and the soul are all one. We are held together by love, and love is so powerful it keeps us together even when you are trying to destroy an aspect of the trilogy…the body. Do you understand?

Me: I…I am overwhelmed. I do understand, God, and am crying tears of joy and gratitude because I hadn't realized just how much You do love me. The idea that my body loves me enough not to fail me even though I'm persecuting it makes so much sense to me. It also makes me terribly remorseful for what I've done. I never wanted to hurt myself, really, I just didn't know I was worthy of my own love. I see now that You love me and are proving to me that Your guidance is always in my best interest. When you explain that my body, You, and I are all one, I can understand for the first time that I can love myself and deserve to. When I love myself, I love You. When I honor my body and respect it, I am honoring and respecting You. And, by honoring and respecting You, I'm also honoring and respecting myself. I GET THIS!!! Oh, God, I really get this. I can really heal and overcome this disease, can't I?

God: Yes, Desmond, you can. You have the power within you. You finally can acknowledge your strength. The amazing thing about healing is the clarity of thought you will receive. Do you realize that much of what you consider your failures actually have resulted from your focus on anorexia and bulimia?

Me: What do you mean?

God: I will give you an example. When you discovered Trinity Lyons had been signed to a recording contract, you thought that you were more deserving and had worked just as hard. It had not been your fault that you had been overlooked. In truth, your focus has not been on your career, your personal relationships, or your spiritual growth. You have focused on your disease for many, many years and have been unable to follow through with total commitment in any area of your life because you have been driven by the compulsive need to starve or binge and purge. As a result, potential opportunities have been lost. A record contract could have easily been given to you if you had committed to the process of accomplishing the goal. You have not been punished. Your free will chose the direction you focused on. The consequence of your decision showed up in this, as well as many other areas. I am telling you this information not to upset you, but to give you encouragement.

When you finally let go of and heal from bulimia, you will be clear-minded and will be able to unite with your body and with love. You will understand and trust My guidance and will accept the opportunities I create. You will know you are worthy of success. You can choose to go up the path of love, and to be of service to love, feeling ultimate joy in fulfilling your purpose by utilizing the gifts I have given you to bless and heal the world. How does all this sound to you?

Me: Oh, God, this sounds like a miracle… an amazing miracle! Will you help me?

God: I am here and will help you. You have asked for a miracle, and you have the power to create one. Believe and trust love.

I was blown away!!! Couldn't believe what I'd just heard...this was the answer I'd needed for twenty years. I had not understood through the anorexia or through the bulimia but now recognized that I'd chosen not to understand during those years. I was truly ready to let go of fear and embrace love!

I'd managed to get out of the doorway and was sitting on the hood of my car by this time. It was a good thing because I was literally weak in the knees and couldn't stand. I looked around to see if anyone was watching me, then eased off my car and got inside.

I'd won the battle! Really won it, for the first time. I'd broken a pattern, and had desired to do so because of love, not fear. It was so powerful!

I put the key in the ignition, started her up, and backed out of the parking space. As I shifted into drive, it dawned on me that I was doing the same actions I'd always done, but now they were different, more alive and present. I looked around while driving and noticed things I'd never seen before. I'd gone down the same streets countless times but had been in a tunnel. This was a new world! It was like I'd just been born and was looking at the planet through clear eyes.

I thought about God, about what I'd been told, and couldn't wait to read this in my *Godtown Guideline Handbook*...wait a minute, Godtown. My heart fluttered. I got it! I understood. I was heading there. Was on my way. I still wasn't sure where it was, but knew it existed, and that I could get to it. This was the right direction...

WHAT A DAY!

I got home from my afternoon and felt compelled to call Julie. I was so excited about what had just happened and wanted to share it with someone. Julie was the only friend who'd understand.

I dialed her number. Her machine picked up, so I left a brief message asking her to call me, then went and started a bath. I thought pampering myself a little was in order. I got candles out, my favorite bubble bath, and turned on a CD of soft jazz music a friend of mine had produced.

As I soaked in my oasis, my mind drifted and started thinking about the concept of God being everywhere and in everyone. It was so cool to imagine being connected to all life in such an intimate way. I wondered if I could reach someone or something through this connection. I decided to ask about it. Why not? True, I was naked and had never been in such an "uncovered" state during one of these talks, but, I mean…geez, I came into this world like that, so why be shy now?

I cleared my mind and asked God to speak to me. As always, the voice was right there, waiting…

God: Desmond, I am always here, twenty-four hours a day, ready to be of loving service to you. To answer your question, yes, you can. Have you heard of prayer?

Me: Well, of course I've heard of prayer.

God: Prayer is the way you can reach out to those you love. It is a sacred communication, and in truth, you are in a form of prayer right now.

Me: Really? This is prayer? Wow, you're kidding me. I always thought prayer was kind of a hit or miss concept. I guess I kind of imagined praying "up" to something that might be floating around in the clouds, and didn't really think it worked.

God: I know. You never utilized prayer until you started listening to Me. Our interaction is actually a very important aspect of prayer. You are becoming open to the words of love and you are starting to live by them. You now can actually send loving prayer out to anyone, anything, and any situation needing your love.

Me: Ok, how do I do that? I know about bowing my head and stuff, but is there any other ritual I have to follow to send prayer?

God: No, you don't have to embrace ritual to send loving prayer out. You don't have to bow your head. You can do so, if you would like, but it is not necessary. You just have to clear your mind, as you do to converse with Me, and direct your thoughts to who and what you want to pray for. Then ask Me to fulfill your prayer. I take your prayer request and deliver it to whoever and whatever you are praying for. It is quite simple. The thing to remember is that prayer is unconditionally love-based and is only effective when your motivations are founded on the loving desire to help and support those in need. Through love. Any prayer that is not love-based is ineffective and, in fact, not prayer.

Me: Well…ok, if I wanted to pray for my brother, let's say, would I just ask you to fulfill my request?

God: What would you like to pray for concerning your brother?

Me: Gosh, well, he's about to step into a new career because he decided to go back to school and get his masters degree in business. He's apprehensive about job prospects in the current business climate. He has a family to support, plus has school loans to repay and is scared he won't be able to find anything. So I'd like to pray for him.

God: Ok, then clear your mind of everything except loving and supportive thoughts for your brother. Ask Me to provide him with the courage to trust

My guidance and the faith to let Me help direct his decisions. Pray for his happiness, well-being, and for him to have an open heart to recognize and believe in his gifts.

Me: I think that's a beautiful prayer, but you know, I haven't been that close to my brother. In fact, I didn't think he liked me that much. Will my prayer still be effective?

God: Every prayer sent through love is effective. Your brother does love you but has not felt you were open to his love. He has thought you have been guarded and somewhat judgmental of his life choices. Both of you have misjudged the other's actions. Judgment cannot be part of a love-based life. Praying for your brother is the first step in the healing of your relationship. He will receive and feel your loving energy.

Me: This is exciting. How does prayer work?

God: I am in everyone and everything. Since all life is a part of Me, and I am a part of you, you are connected to all life through Me. There is a phenomenon called the Internet, which you are familiar with. It not only gives you access to a wealth of information, it also connects all the computers of the world together. People can interact with each other by typing messages on their computer and sending them through the system to another person's computer. Prayer is a similar concept. Think of everyone and everything as being connected by a giant, invisible web. I am the connector. Everyone and everything is accessible through Me. Prayer is your keypad, so to speak. You can create a prayer, send it through Me, and I will deliver the love to the recipient. Your prayer is effective because it is love in motion. There is nothing more powerful than loving energy.

Me: God, this makes sense to me, but how do you do that, you know, make my prayer effective in my brother's life? How do you get him to accept my prayer?

God: I hesitate to make something as holy as prayer a comparison to a computer system, but the concepts are vaguely similar. This can show you, in a simplistic manner, how your prayer can reach its recipient. As you know, when you send a message through the computer system, the person who receives it has the option to read it or ignore it. It is his or her free will choice. So it is with prayer. If your heart is open to love, prayer can flow into your soul and you feel its power immediately. If your heart is closed and full of fear, though, prayer will still touch you because it is in your "terminal." The message will wait for you to open it. The prayer will never delete. In other words, it will stay in "unopened mail" forever, if necessary. It will also continue to send out a signal to the recipient that it is waiting for him or her to open it. It "beeps" and eventually the hope is that the "beep" will be acknowledged and the message will be received. I need to state that it is a much more holy, powerful experience than what I have just illustrated for you, but I want you to understand, in simplistic terms, how real prayer is. Trust it is among the most powerful expressions of love you can give.

Me: Thank you for explaining prayer in such an easily understood manner. I do get this and am excited about trying it out. Oh, by the way, can we send my brother's prayer to him?

God: Yes. It is done.

Me: Thank you. I guess you realize how simple minded I am, but that's ok because I appreciate your efforts to converse with me in a way I will get the message. Do you ever feel like you are writing for a teen magazine?

God: Desmond, you are amusing. I speak in a way you will understand based on where you are in your journey.

Me: Ok, I get it. I was....

The phone rang and distracted me. I reached over with dripping hand and grabbed it. Julie was on the other line. I was very excited to hear her voice and proceeded to tell her about the day's events. When I got to the part about the battle to "bury the pain," though, I suddenly hesitated because I hadn't shared my struggle of bulimia or anorexia with her before. I brilliantly stalled (I thought) by asking to call her right back because I was turning into a prune in the bathtub. She said sure, but to hurry because she couldn't wait to hear the rest of my story.

I hung the phone up and proceeded to get out of the tub. This was a big crossroads. I'd never admitted my disease or my struggles to anyone before. How could I do this? I got very nervous and actually started shaking...ok, some of that probably was caused from being dripping wet... but it was also because I was scared to be vulnerable with her. Afraid of judgment. Afraid...fear...I was jumping to a conclusion based on my fear. Julie had acknowledged her inner voice and had seemed open to exploring a relationship with it, so if anyone could be open and accepting of my frailties, it would be Julie.

I dried off, got dressed, and decided to call her back. After she answered, she excitedly begged me to continue my story. So I did but explained that there were some details to fill her in on, first. After I told her the whole deal, the entire background of my battle with anorexia and bulimia, she was silent on the other end of the phone. I panicked for a minute thinking she was repulsed by my admission, but then she said something that shocked me.

"Desmond, my cousin Shelly died because she was anorexic. She literally starved herself to death. Until my brother's death, it was the most devastating experience my family has ever gone through. None of us understood why she did that to herself. None of us could help her. In a way, it was harder to accept than my brother's death because it could've been completely avoided."

My jaw dropped! Unbelievable. Julie had never mentioned her cousin before, but I guess the loss was a very confusing experience for her. I said, "Julie, I'm so sorry. I didn't know you had lost someone you loved to this disease. Do you want me to continue?"

"Oh, yes!" she exclaimed. "Maybe you will help shed some light on why Shelly couldn't save herself. I've never been able to accept the fact she allowed herself to die."

I replied, "Julie, Shelly didn't think she had a choice. She was so full of fear that she was drowning in it. She felt powerless because she thought the disease was bigger than she was. She also felt extremely alone, even though you and the rest of your family were around her. When you're trapped in anorexia, it's like being locked in a very small safe. You can't move. You can't even turn over. You believe you'll be imprisoned forever because you think the lock that opens the door is on the outside. You can't reach it because you're inside. What an anorexic doesn't realize is that the safe isn't locked. In fact, there's not even a lock on it. It only requires pushing the door open and stepping out, but no one tells you it's that easy because everyone else assumes it's locked too. No one encourages you to try to push from the inside because they don't understand what the safe even is or how it works. In fact, they're confused about how you got inside it in the first place. Even if they could understand, you wouldn't accept their help because you've pushed them away in the past. You don't trust anyone and think they are jealous of you for being so thin, so you never listen to them. As a result, you remain in the dark, scared and lonely.

The truth is, help doesn't come from the outside. The key to freedom comes from within. It will come from your voice of love, from God, if you have the courage to listen. It's confusing, though, because you've had another voice inside of you saying how horrible and disgusting you are. It says you're so stupid that you can't save yourself. You don't believe the voice of love because you're so conditioned to listening to the negative voice, which is the one *you* created from your lack of self-worth. It seems logical to listen to the negative voice because it validates what you've heard from people around you for years. How could they be wrong? You don't think you have a right to listen to the voice of love...that is, if you're even aware of it. It's buried under immense fear. You're afraid to trust your body and your love voice because you've made them the enemy. Your thinking is completely backwards. You've given the voice of fear the respect you should be giving to the voice of love. That's why you're in the safe. Even if someone tries to tell you about the healing ability of God, you won't listen because you think they're trying to sabotage you.

So it goes until you feel it's too late. You wither up and die because you don't believe you can escape. You're too afraid to try to push the door open because you think you'll fail if you attempt to do so anyway, so why bother. You give up. At least that's what I felt like when I was anorexic. The only reason I ended up coming out of the disease was because I had a few circumstances that forced me to change my behavior. I became anemic, broke my foot, and had a metabolic meltdown all at the same time. I mean, I ended up jumping over to bulimia, but didn't die from anorexia. I feel reasonably certain I could have, though. Does any of this make sense, Julie?"

"Yes, it does," she answered. "It's so tragic to think Shelly didn't realize she had a choice to listen to God. Why could she not hear her loving voice?"

I said, "Why could we not hear the voice of God for so long? We were just as full of fear as Shelly was. I don't know why we ended up opening our hearts, and she didn't. I wish I could answer that question, but your inner voice could help you understand Shelly's fear. Have you been talking to God?"

Julie said, "Yeah, I have. I'm amazed how differently I feel about life. I'm actually starting to become sincerely happy, walking around with a grin on my face all the time. There are things I haven't covered yet, but I really believe God is inside me and that this voice is love. I'll talk to God about Shelly's death because I miss her very much and have never really gotten over it. Thanks for trying to help me understand...now, finish your story about what happened today."

So I did, and we talked for another hour about it. She knew Trinity Lyons also, and was surprised at the signing, but her reaction was more gracious than mine had been. Julie was definitely a special person. I really liked her a lot and was happy we were going through this experience at the same time and were becoming closer because of it.

We ended our talk by agreeing to have dinner together over the weekend. After I hung up, I wanted to get back to discussing prayer with God but checked my messages earlier and had received a call from a man I'd met a couple of weeks before. I'd forgotten he'd asked me to dinner, so when I picked up his reminder message, I thought about canceling but realized it was too late. What the heck, I guess I could go. I'd agreed to meet him at a great restaurant by the beach, so at least it would be a nice dinner...that sounds awful, doesn't it? Well, it's just that first dates are always kind of uncomfortable and chances are they won't work out, so I never got my hopes up. I tried to be very pragmatic and look at things very logically and then, by a long shot, if I actually found myself attracted, I was pleasantly surprised. There, now I hope it doesn't sound like I was callous. I just wasn't projecting anything...ok, anyway, I pulled myself together by throwing my hair up and changing clothes, then hopped in the car and headed down to the beach.

Man, what a day I'd gone through. So much had transpired. I'd turned a corner and stress was just nowhere to be found. How could it have dissipated so quickly? I knew the answer and was awe-struck by the power of God and love.

I got to the restaurant and the valet took my car. I was walking up to the door when all of a sudden I couldn't remember what this guy looked like. I knew he was cute, but it had been a couple of weeks and we'd only had a brief conversation in a crowded room. Luckily, there were only two men sitting in the bar area when I walked in. My date recognized me immediately, so the problem was solved. (Hmmm, he was cuter than I'd remembered!) He took my hand, lightly kissed my cheek, and told me I looked beautiful. I actually even believed him, sort of, which was surprising because compliments were usually very difficult for me to accept. I'd pretend to, but inside I'd cringe! I thanked him and said he looked quite nice, himself. He escorted me over to a table in the bar and asked if I'd like a drink. I answered that a Chardonnay would be nice, so he went to get me one. I tried to remember his full name. Mark was his first, but the last name escaped me. I decided to try to somehow secretly finagle it out of him before the night was over. (Does it surprise you I'd meet a man for dinner who I didn't really know? Well, I have to say I was a pro when it came to dating but was very careful about who I'd accept this kind of date with. If I met the guy at a friend's party and my friend approved, then I'd feel pretty safe about going out with him. I met Mark in one of those situations. I gotta tell you, though, a girl can never be too careful!)

Anyway, we chatted and I discovered he had a keen wit. He made me laugh almost every time he said something. How fun. The hostess came over and told us our table was ready, so we moved into the restaurant and were seated by a window with a beautiful ocean view. How nice was this!?! I was having a great time. I was my flirtatious self but felt more real and centered instead of performing, like I usually did in situations like this. I think it showed because he seemed to enjoy himself, too. We had a terrific dinner, and the truth is, I didn't even worry about what I was eating. I was actually present at the table and with him, and didn't give the meal a second thought. Now *that* hadn't happened in twenty years. This was unbelievable! We ended the evening by agreeing to go out again very soon.

I retrieved my car from valet, and Mark opened my door for me. Then he took my hand, raised it to his lips, and lightly kissed it. (Wow...cool...a gentleman!) He told me he had a wonderful time and that he'd call me the next day. I wouldn't hold my breath for the call but was impressed with him. (I think I was reverting back to some Humanville thinking, but had learned enough in my single years to not put much credence in a man's word early on. He'd have to prove his sincerity, but we'd see. I decided to check in with God later and find out how one approaches dating in the "world of love." I'd only dated in "fear land" in the past. Oh, by the way, his last name was Henderson.) I pulled away from the restaurant with a smile on my face. Can't say I was head-over-heels crazy about him, but I did think he was a good guy. I drove home in a great mood.

Getting ready for bed, I hesitated in my routine a second and remembered what I'd learned about prayer. I decided to give thanks for a special day. I cleared my mind and told God how much I appreciated love's guidance, and suddenly a really cool thing happened. I glanced in the mirror, and for a brief moment (I promise you), saw a little glow emanating from my face. I don't think I imagined it. I really saw an illumination! Faint, mind you, but it was there. I just smiled to myself, finished my prayer, and went to bed. What a day! Couldn't wait for the next one...

OH, THIS IS HOW IT WORKS!

For the next two weeks I awoke everyday with a newfound peace and happiness. I was focusing on just taking one moment at a time and living through love. As a result, I was becoming a healthy, normal person and could eat a meal with confidence and without worry. I was continually amazed with the power of love. I was finally free from my twenty-year prison. As long as I chose love, I'd continue to live the miracle.

Going through my coffee routine one morning, I decided to say hi to God. I'd made a habit of starting the day in this manner and was stepping out on the "good foot," as they say. Since I hadn't seriously focused on work since the "Lou and Trinity showdown," I thought I finally should direct my attention to this subject. I cleared my mind and greeted my voice with bountiful enthusiasm. I received a loving salutation.

God: Hello, Desmond, you are feeling very chipper this morning. I am very happy you are starting your mornings with Me. You trust yourself more and more. This is a wonderful experience for you.

Me: Yes, I feel terrific! Whatever You're doing, I sure like the results of your efforts!

God: You are benefiting from what you have done and from your efforts, also. We have accomplished much together, and this is just the beginning for you.

Me: Yep, I understand this. So, listen, I figure I'll just avoid any major disaster today and come straight to you for guidance...you know, on the front end. I need to ask for help in finding the correct career direction and for a way to generate immediate income. I don't want to panic but do need to be able to cover my expenses. I want to keep away from as much modeling as possible because I really don't want my image to be plastered in too many cheesy magazines and be overexposed. I'd consider a major publication—you know, high-end fashion or something like that— but otherwise would rather focus on music. I think a great studio gig, other than Tiffany's record, would generate pretty good immediate income. And there are the future performance and mechanical royalties, which always help...

God: Desmond, look what you are doing. You are completely ignoring love and service and focusing on a self-absorbed pattern of control that will only lead to disappointment and failure. Everything you've gone through with Me is being completely buried right now by the same fear that has always driven you. When it comes to your career, you are very afraid. You are not asking for guidance, you are dictating what you think is the direction you want to go. You are still thinking inside your box.

Me: Well, I don't know how to do this! I thought I was supposed to come to you for help and guidance. Are you now telling me I'm wrong?

God: No, I am reminding you that you are here to serve the universe and share your love and gifts to aid in the healing of the world. It is not an issue of what will serve you. My guidance will help you find your path to serve others, which, in turn, will completely fulfill you. Let go of your fear and insecurity. You do not have to prove your worth to anybody. You are complete because you are loved by Me and now know you can love yourself. You are realizing you can love others just as unconditionally through Me. So, I ask you to try again. Get out of your own way and go to love.

Me: Ok, that hit a nerve. However, I can't argue with what you're telling me. I just don't know what I'm doing in the "land of love" yet. I know, I know, listen and just be open to You, right?

God: Yes, right.

Me: Ok, I'll try again. God, I ask you to guide me down the path of love today and give me the wisdom to choose love in every situation I experience and in every moment I live. I ask specifically to be shown to my road of service and to be blessed with the ability to generate income. I ask you to watch over my loved ones and keep them in your light, and I ask you to stay in the forefront of my heart and soul today and shine through me...How's that?

God: Desmond, you prayed a very beautiful, love-filled prayer. Did it feel different to you than the first one?

Me: Yes, absolutely. It didn't feel selfish and self-absorbed. I got out of my own way and it just came out. Wow, cool.

God: Yes, it is "cool" as you say. Stay with Me today, and you will experience blessing after blessing.

Me: Ok, I'll give 'er a try! Now what do I do?

God: Start your day.

Me: Yes, of course. That's the same thing you've said every morning. By the way, You're right about my career focus. I do bring out negative energy when I start to think about it. Thank you for pointing this out to me. I'll be open to Your guidance today, God, that's a promise. All right... Here it goes!

I finished my coffee and jumped in the shower. I had to do some errands, so after dressing and getting ready, I headed out. My first stop was the dry cleaners to pick up the clothes I'd left two days before. Then I went and put gas in my car. While I was standing at the pump, I looked over to the next one, and there stood Bruce Webster. I knew Bruce because he owned one of the more successful studios in Humanville, called Magnolia. I'd worked at his place quite a few times and really liked the facility. We greeted each other and I told him he looked great, then asked how he'd been. He said he was going crazy because the studio had been totally booked for the last four months. (I found his statement a little amusing because Magnolia was always booked. In fact, it was almost impossible to get in there without a long wait.) He said he'd been very hands-on with the current project because it was a record being produced by Steve Barham. Steve Barham!?! He was one of the biggest producers in music! His focus was mostly mainstream rock, but he was really into diversifying, so he'd take on unique projects from time to time. Bruce excitedly told me about what Steve was working on. Apparently, it was an album of very hip and esoteric songs that used a full orchestra, but also all kinds of special sounds and instruments from all over the world. For instance, the current song they were cutting utilized war drums—from a primitive tribe of people who lived in the jungle—a harpsichord, a sitar, and an ancient instrument called a hurdy-gurdy. It was over 1000 years old and sounded like a cross between a violin and bagpipe. All on one production number. I couldn't imagine what it could possibly sound like and said so to Bruce. He replied by telling me that I should hear for myself, and invited me to come to the studio and listen to it.

Wow, I jumped at the invitation! To see Steve Barham work in the flesh was an unbelievably exciting opportunity. Bruce told me to just follow him over.

When we got to the studio, he led me into the control room. (This is where the console is and where the engineer and producer oversee the musicians and singers during a recording session.) They were in the middle of listening to a track they had just cut, so I stood quietly and listened, also. Wild! It was the most awesome sound! The music gave me chills, but more than that, I felt a peace which was similar to the feeling I'd get after I'd have a talk with God. It was really cool because I was already in that space because of my morning interaction, but this music was bringing me to an even higher place. I closed my eyes and drank in the sound. What were they doing here? I had to know.

Just then, the music stopped. I opened my eyes at the precise moment Steve Barham turned around to face me. I almost jumped back because he had it! The glow...the one I'd seen in the two people at the coffee shop and in the old woman who gave me the *Godtown Guideline Handbook*! I just stared at him and couldn't take my eyes off his face. He smiled at me, then winked at the engineer and told him it sounded great. He patted the guy on the back, turned to Bruce and said, "So, who is this lovely person you have graced our presence with, Bruce?" (He was referring to me, although for some reason I couldn't believe he'd described me as lovely...he was the glowing one!)

Bruce introduced me and I stumbled over my words and managed to say something profound like "nice to meet you." I was mesmerized, so I'm sure I came across as a groupie, or something. Steve took my hand and welcomed me to "his world," and then introduced his engineer, Mike, to me. I said that I hoped this wasn't an intrusion, and Steve replied, "Not at all."

He proceeded to explain that what I'd just heard was a dream come true for him. He'd desired to create an album of spiritual music for many years but had not been free to do so because of other work obligations. He'd finally just put his foot down and refused other projects because he knew the time had come for him to do this one. He explained he'd been led to create the album and that it had fallen into place in a matter of weeks because every door just opened up. Even this studio had been booked, but because of a cancellation, became available at the last minute. He wanted to work in Magnolia because it had been converted into a studio out of an old church. He thought it had very positive energy.

I didn't know what to say! I must have been staring at him because Bruce interjected at this point and explained who I was. He told Steve I'd worked on numerous albums singing background vocals and Steve's eyes lit up with interest. He asked if I'd worked with anyone he might know and I told him I'd just finished singing on the latest Focus Cain album. Focus Cain was a hot, alternative rock band that had hit big on their freshman album. They had sold something like three million units, so everyone was curious about what their sophomore effort would sound like. (I personally thought it was a cooler album than the first, but was more evolved musically, so I wasn't sure how the public would react.) Steve seemed impressed at this part of my resume and mentioned that I must be a good singer. I responded by saying I had a pretty strong harmony ear and was quick in the studio. I was a little embarrassed talking about myself because I was such a peon compared to him, but he seemed sincerely interested in what I was saying. (You know, this was not a sexual attraction I had for him. It was something I'd never experienced before. It was...I don't know...a spiritual connection, like I'd known him for a long time. I was certain that I'd never met him, though. He wasn't a classically handsome man, but his energy made him beautiful.)

I apparently daydreamed for a second because all of a sudden I heard Bruce say, "Desmond, isn't that great?" I shook my head and stammered, " Oh, uh, yeah, that's great!" I had no idea what I was talking about, but must have agreed to something terrific because everyone was smiling.

Steve said, "Well, wonderful, then. If you could just drop it by the studio later today, I will listen and let you know tomorrow, ok?"

I said, "Sure." Then Bruce said he had to run upstairs, so I took that as a hint to leave myself. I thanked Steve for letting me eavesdrop on their session and stated that it had been nice to meet him. He returned the compliment and said he'd look forward to seeing me later in the day.

As we walked out the door, I turned to Bruce and asked, "What in the world did I just agree to do?" Bruce laughed and said, "Desmond, come on! You just want me to gloat over you because Steve Barham wants to listen to your demo to check out your voice."

I froze. "He does?" I questioned.

"You were standing right there when he asked to hear it. Boy, you really were starstruck, weren't you!?!" he exclaimed.

Yeah, I guess I had been. I laughed it off with Bruce and said I was just trying to get him to dote on me, but inside I was shocked! This was what God was talking about when He said to have faith and trust love's guidance. I didn't plan or plot any of this but tried to keep centered and love-based. It had just flowed. I mean, I had no idea why Steve Barham wanted to hear my voice, but was extremely flattered he even asked for a CD.

I patted Bruce on the arm, told him I'd drop my demo by later in the day, and thanked him profusely for introducing me to Steve. He said it was his pleasure to be of service to me, waved bye, and ran up the stairs. Be of service...he'd said be of service. Bruce was a very kind man, and you know, he had a light inside of him, also. Had I not noticed it before? I wondered if Bruce had found his inner voice and lived through love. It certainly seemed as if he did. And I knew Steve Barham had an incredible light! I couldn't wait to come back later.

I finished my errands, then ran home to grab my CD. I quickly checked my messages (nothing too important), freshened up, and decided to get a quick bite to eat before I went back to the studio. I made a sandwich and poured some iced tea. I cleaned the kitchen and then...hey, wait a minute. It had happened again. I'd eaten a meal, even in my own house, and had not fretted over it. It seemed like the most natural thing in the world. I wasn't driven by an obsessive need to overdo the eating thing. This was a true miracle!

I finished cleaning, then jumped back in the car and headed to Magnolia. I thought about the fact I'd now gone through two weeks of eating in a very normal way and was ecstatic. Does it seem bizarre to you I'd be so excited about something as mundane as eating a sandwich? Well, let me tell you, parting the world's biggest ocean would not have been more of a miracle for me. This was huge! I'd broken out of prison. I'd pushed the door open and realized that there had been no lock. It had been that easy. It had also been the most extraordinary challenge I'd ever overcome.

I went back into the control room when I got to the studio, and unfortunately, Steve and Mike had taken a lunch break. I just left my CD on the console with a little note and left the building. I'd hoped to get to talk to him again, but didn't get disappointed, I just let God take the situation from there, and didn't worry about the outcome. I'd never thought this way before. I was appreciating the opportunity to meet Steve, enjoying the process of the day, and surprising myself with my centered attitude...but I knew it was more than that. God was guiding me...

STEVE'S STORY

I didn't hear from Steve Barham for a week and a half. I wasn't surprised because when someone in music land says, "I'll let you know tomorrow" it means at least a week, if not longer. Just the way it is. I'd gone about my business and had kept God right up front. As a result, I hadn't worried about not hearing from him and had been reassured I was "experiencing the process" really well. The cool thing is, I hadn't turned to bulimia once and felt very normal. In the past, I would've reacted to this silent period by taking it personally and then "burying the rejection." It would've gotten worse every day that passed until I became hopeless and repulsed. Now, I was really living life in a way I'd only been able to dream about before.

When I got Steve's message, I played it three times in a row and was totally enchanted by what he said. It went something like this...

"Desmond, darling, hello." (He called me "darling," how endearing!)
"Steve Barham, here. I first want to apologize for not calling in a timely
manner after I told you I would do so." (He's apologizing to me, wow!)
"You so kindly left your CD and I desperately desired to listen to it
immediately." (It's ok, really. You don't have to pretend you wanted to that
much). "Unfortunately, we had some complications in the studio with
equipment meltdown and what not, and I was somewhat tied up with
untangling a small web of chaos because of it." (I know that's a real
possibility. It's a typical day in the studio). "Nonetheless, I hope you did
not give up on me." (Like I would *ever* give up on you!). "I just want you to
know I finally had the honor of listening to your demo and thought it was
truly wonderful." (You've got to be kidding me! Really?) "I love the
sound and tonality of your voice. It has almost an angelic quality to it." (I
am *melting* here!) "I actually was wondering if you could be so kind to
return my call, for I'd like to talk to you further about this in person. You
can reach me at the studio, or my beeper number is 555-5487." (He is giving
my his private beeper number!?! I can't believe this!) "I hope to hear from
you in the near future. Take care. Bye"

I was thrilled, but didn't react in my usual way. I was flattered by his
message but felt a sincerity behind it that made more of an impact on me. I
knew he wasn't playing a game. He meant what he was saying, I could tell.
Usually, I'd second guess the words and end up feeling bad about everything
because I'd put a double meaning into what I heard. This was very
different.

I went ahead and called the studio. He was in session, so I left a message on his beeper. He called back ten minutes later and invited me to come down to Magnolia that afternoon. I said I'd be there, hung up, and went to get myself ready, which, I admit took close to two hours because I tried on every single piece of clothing in my closet, looking for the "perfect" thing to wear (some things never change!) I took off to meet him never looking better, in my opinion. (Obviously, I hadn't conquered the image thing, yet!)

When I arrived, Steve took one look at me and said as sincerely as he could, "Well, Desmond, how lovely you look. You must have attended a black tie luncheon prior to coming here. You are certainly putting the rest of us to shame in the style department. I feel absolutely shabby next to you." (Ok, it figures—I overdid it!). I replied by saying that yes, I'd been at a previous engagement. (So it had been in my closet. That counts, doesn't it?) He asked if I'd mind waiting a few minutes. They were finishing up an overdub and would be through very soon. I said sure, and sat down on the couch. I loved watching him work! It was artistry in motion. He literally crawled into the music and became a part of it. He lost himself in the sound and I could tell he was listening to every note, every string, every beat, and every nuance.

Finally, they finished the track and he turned, motioning me to follow him out of the control room. I did as asked and almost had to run to catch up. He walked extremely fast and had a bounce in his step that propelled him even more rapidly. We ended up in the lounge area, and he suggested we go out to have a cup of coffee. He said he could use a little fresh air. I offered to drive and he took me up on it because he admitted he was not the best driver in the world and didn't want to endanger my life. He was joking, but I had a feeling there was a bit of truth behind his statement. So, we got in my car and I took him to a coffee shop near the studio. Ironically, we ended up at the very same place I'd been in when I first encountered the "glowing people" I've told you about. We went in, ordered, and found a table near the back.

As we sat down, he expressed how much he appreciated me taking the time to come meet him. I thought, "Like I had to rearrange my calendar for Steve Barham!!" I smiled back and said it was my pleasure and added I was flattered he even listened to my CD. His eyes lit up at that statement, and he excitedly told me he was intrigued with the sound of my voice. I said in a most eloquent fashion, "Really?" (I know, it's sad, isn't it? Such a limited vocabulary!)

He said, "Yes, Desmond, really!"

I thanked him and he then continued, "You know, I took your demo home and played it for my wife and daughters and they agreed that you have the most angelic tonality to your voice."

I thought he was married, for I'd read an article about him once that had talked about how strong his relationship was. I remember thinking he and his wife must be special people to maintain a solid marriage in *this* industry.

I was flattered he felt so positive about my CD. He kindly pointed out that I could've used some stronger material to showcase my voice but that it had been easy to hear through the songs, anyway. (He didn't know I'd written or co-written all the material on the CD, but I didn't take offense because I knew he was right. I'd thought the same thing but had not replaced any songs because I hadn't finished the new project Lou had invested in and...ok, better not go there. I was trying to forgive Lou, but still slipped into the Humanville thought process concerning him. God was definitely letting me know I needed to focus on love and let it go...ugh!) I shook my head in affirmation, so he knew he hadn't offended me.

He continued. "Desmond, I'd like to use you in one of the songs I'm working on. In fact, it's the one you heard last week when you came in the studio with Bruce."

"Wow, Steve, I don't quite know what to say. I loved that song. It was the most fascinating, haunting, beautiful, and overwhelming piece of music I've ever heard! " I exclaimed.

He replied, "Thank you. I feel the same way. I can't take credit for it because it was truly a gift. I was just chosen to deliver the gift to the world."

I looked at him and could not contain myself. I was trying to keep this meeting professional, but couldn't just let the moment pass without bringing up this question. I hesitated for only a second, then looked him straight in the eyes and asked, "Where did the gift come from?"

His response was, "Well, where all gifts of love come from...it came from God."

A huge smile spread across my face because I could talk to this man and he'd know exactly what I was referring to. I cleared my throat and then proceeded. "Steve, why did you just ask me to sing on your record?"

He looked at me and did not hesitate, blink an eye, or feel awkward in any way. He said with conviction, "Because I was told to...you were brought to me through prayer. I didn't have to seek you out, God provided you to me. All I did was ask for the right voice to come to me and next thing I know, you're standing right behind me in the studio."

All I could do was just stare at him with the "deer in headlights" look.

When I didn't respond, Steve continued. "I learned a long time ago to listen to my inner voice and trust its guidance. Believe me, there was a time I didn't, and it wasn't pretty. My life was a mess. I'm even surprised I survived those years."

I said, "I'm so amazed you'd even consider me to be on a project you're creating. I'd be honored to work with you. I want you to know this, because I hope you don't mind—and please tell me if this is being intrusive—but I'm wondering if you could tell me about how you discovered your inner voice and God."

Steve smiled and replied, "No, I don't mind. It's my greatest accomplishment, really. I'd normally say my children and marriage are my best achievements, but they are also a part of God, so it all ties together. I'm assuming you're asking me because you are going through a metamorphosis and recognize I might have been through the same tunnel, right? Well, I'll tell you about my trip from darkness to light, if it will help you understand what you're going through. I'm not usually so candid because in Humanville it's hard to understand how I perceive life, but I don't hide any aspect of who I am, either. I do know many people judge how I live, but hopefully I'll still touch them in some way. If I can help someone else find love from within, then I'll gladly bear every detail of my life to them."

I responded, "I'd appreciate hearing your story. You're right, I am going through a tremendous shift in my life and really can't believe I found someone like you to talk to."

Steve said, "Ahh, Desmond, that's where you are mistaken. You should absolutely *expect* to find someone like me when you need to. This is how love works and how God will guide you if you're open to it. Do you realize you were supposed to come to the studio last week? You were supposed to meet me and I was supposed to meet you. Life is so easy when you let it be. Do you understand what I'm talking about?"

I replied, "Sort of. This is all very new to me, so I don't know quite how to react to everything. I'm trying to learn to trust my inner voice of love and am excited about what has changed in my life, but I've only been able to talk to one friend about this, who is going through the same experience. I still get so confused at times."

Steve listened, then was quiet for a minute. I sat there waiting for him to respond, but he just kept staring at me with this look on his face that was a cross between a smile and an inquisitive gleam. Have you seen someone with that kind look before? You don't quite know what they're thinking. Usually it's unsettling, but in this case I wasn't bothered by it. In fact, I was touched because he was so genuine.

He finally spoke, "I know exactly how you feel. I remember being at a crossroads in life and was aware of the path to love, but I was conditioned to live in fear. It seemed impossible to change the way I did things. I didn't believe I could do it. Nor did I really want to do it, at first. I enjoyed the party. The drugs, women, alcohol, sex...the whole thing, really.

"I thought I was on top of the world when I first started becoming successful as a producer. I was in my early twenties and had worked with my first band for a few years. It just so happened I'd started out in the band but realized early on that my talent was in producing. The guys didn't want me to quit playing. I made a deal with them to still be a part of the group, but as their producer, since none of them really had the gift like I did. I enjoyed it so much more than playing. I didn't mind not being on stage and, in fact, appreciated not having to perform. I was actually shy but would never admit that. I made everyone believe I was sacrificing my artist career to become the band's producer. I was so convincing that I became a god in their eyes. In truth, I was scared to death of failure every minute of every day.

In an attempt to hide my fear, I played the part of a king and started riding an amazing high. Then I bought into it. I had power and loved it!

"We had achieved a reasonable amount of success on our side of the ocean, but wanted to break into the bigger league, so we started coming here and slowly gained recognition. The breakthrough for us was the 'Winged Heart' album. Maybe you remember it."

I couldn't believe he'd just asked me that question. You see, the band he was talking about was Mammoth, one of the biggest rock bands in the history of music. They had become huge in the early-seventies and had ridden on top of the charts for over twenty years. Everyone knew the reason they'd made it so big was because of Steve's talent. He was a genius and even the band members gave him the credit—which is unusual for big egos. Yes, I remembered it, and told him so.

He continued, "Well, you were very young then, so I wasn't sure. Anyhow, things moved very quickly after that album and I rode the wave in fine fashion. Made a lot of money, and spent a lot of money. It was all about show, all about image. I found myself in what now seems like unbelievable situations, but at the time I thought I was untouchable. I won't bore you with the details. Mine's a pretty typical story in the music business. The more successful I became, the further I slipped into the depths of Humanville."

~

I didn't interrupt him because I was enthralled with what he was sharing with me. I haven't mentioned that Steve had the most beautiful accent. It was lilting, warm, and very proper. He definitely was from across the ocean. I could've listened to him talk for hours, not even caring about what he was saying. Since I recognized he was giving me insight into his life, though, and was selflessly opening up his personal experience to help me, I was very grateful and impressed with his candor, so I paid attention.

He continued, "I'd lived in Humanville my entire life and hadn't the foggiest idea I could see the world through any other perspective than anger, fear, greed, and selfishness. My childhood was wrought with physical abuse and mental torment. My father was a very unhappy man and had a mental breakdown when I was twelve. I believe this was caused from the death of his father, who'd been a tyrant but who dad had nonetheless idolized. He never got the approval he so desperately needed from his father and had rebelled when he was a teen. The two of them never healed their relationship, so when Grandfather died, my dad just fell apart. That's when the worst years of abuse began for me. I think my dad had to vent his pain and anguish and I was the closest target. I tried and tried to make my dad feel better, but couldn't fix him. I blamed myself for his suffering and then thought I deserved his abuse because I could not take his pain away. A vicious five-year battle ensued. I finally couldn't take the torture anymore, so I ran away. I was seventeen at the time and thought I could take care of myself.

"I found solace in my guitar and in making music. My sanctuary became this music club I hung out in day after day. I'd bring my guitar and the in-house band would let me sit in with them. Music was my only refuge from the streets of Humanville. It was a tough world and no one cared about a young, seventeen-year-old kid who didn't have a pot to piss in.

"I learned how to work the streets very quickly. I found heroin and cocaine, and before long I was not only using but also selling. I became a businessman and started making a lot of money pushing whatever I could get my hands on. I was living in the bowels of the city, and it was a nightmare, but I survived. Only the music kept me from suffering the same kind of nervous breakdown my dad fell victim to. I was arrested once and incarcerated for a period of one month. I got out on a technicality, which to this day I don't quite understand. I turned around and hit the streets again immediately.

"The club I hung out in also attracted other young, hungry musicians. This is where I met Tommy Burns, Claude Montaine, and Jesse Colburn. All of us were in the same boat—lost, scared, and hungry. Fortunately, we also had another common bond. We all possessed some musical talent. We started jamming together and eventually jelled into a cohesive band. We named ourselves 'Mammoth' because the club we jammed in had a big picture of one hanging on the wall. The name seemed to fit our dreams, so we adopted it.

"We started playing around our part of the city and created a small buzz. One night, a fellow from an independent record label wandered into the club and introduced himself to us after our first set. His name was Gerome Guidro. He gave us his card and asked us to call him the next day. We did, and the next thing you know, we'd signed our first record contract. We had no idea what we were doing, but luckily Gerome was greedy and slick enough to actually get our record on the radio, and we got played on some mid-level stations. The turning point for us was the day James Horner, who owned Authority Records, just happened to be channel-surfing on his car radio and accidentally overheard our record on one of these stations. He flipped over the song, had his staff track us down, showed up on our doorstep a week later, and offered us a buyout from Gerome, plus a very lucrative deal on Authority. We jumped at the offer and before we knew it, we were the biggest band on our side of the ocean.

"I got caught up with the whole thing. Obviously, I'd left drug pushing behind by that time but was a professional user. Man, I couldn't quit. Every high had to be higher. I became an intravenous junkie around the time we started recording the 'Winged Heart' album. I justified my addiction by saying it made me more creative. I knew I was full of bull, but apparently other people bought the excuse because I even finagled the record company to include supplying me with coke and heroin as part of my contract. They gladly obliged. I was making them millions and millions of dollars, and they knew the guys in the band regarded me as the "patriarch" and would do anything I said to do. So, they figured 'if we keep Steve happy, we keep everybody happy!' They were right, except that they didn't take into consideration the fact that I was so lost in my addiction. I finally overdosed and almost died. Should have died, really. Why I was spared, I didn't know. I came out of the fog lying in a hospital bed, tubes sticking out of every part of my body. Apparently, I'd been driving my Farrari when I went into my blackout. I wrecked and broke enough bones to keep me incapacitated for four months. There were many times I wished I had died. The pain was excruciating. Not to mention the fact I could no longer get my drug fix, so when the doctors cut back on my pain medication, I went into major drug withdrawal.

"Desmond, it was the darkest time in my life. All I could do was lie there in my bed and think. I was angry, scared, and lonely because the only real friends I had were Tommy, Jesse, and Claude. They came to see me as much as they could but were touring all over the place and just couldn't break away very often.

"The media kept close vigil, but they were hoping I'd croak so they'd have an attention-getting headline for their publications. I mean, it was bad. Some of them would masquerade as doctors and nurses so they could get by the security men the label had provided for me. One time, two of them got as far as my bed and snapped a photo before security could get them out. I wouldn't be surprised if you saw the picture. It was in every news publication around the world. I looked like a living corpse and I think most of the captions described me as such.

"Even though it was my bleakest hour, a miracle was given to me that changed my life. In the depths of depression and despair, there was one person who became a friend of mine. Her name was Judith, and she was one of my nurses. At first, I was the worst patient in the world—bossy, demanding, impetuous. Judith was so patient with me and so nurturing to me, I eventually softened my attitude when she came into my room. Eventually, I found myself looking forward to her shift because she made me feel better about, well, everything, really. She had this amazing glow that lit up my room when she entered. I couldn't describe it at the time, but I knew she was a very special person. She started out being very "nursely" to me but slowly opened up and shared some of her heart with me and listened patiently for sometimes hours while I poured out mine to her. I trusted her, for some reason, and grew to love her in a very pure way.

"Please understand I was not sexually attracted to Judith. She was actually fifty-four years old at the time. I thought that maybe she represented a mother figure to me. I'd lost my own mum when I was five. I didn't tell you that part, did I? Yes…died of cancer shortly after she gave birth to my younger brother. I missed her terribly, but realized Judith was someone unique in my life, and was a soulmate in a way.

"As I healed, Judith started telling me about a part of her life that was very sacred. She told me about finding God and how she was led to her path of service. She explained she had been very unhappy at one point because she was a single mother raising two children and was not making it. She fell to her knees one night in exhaustion and despair and heard, through her pain, a whisper calling her name. She looked around the room, but realized the whisper was inside her own mind. When she finally acknowledged it, she found her inner voice and God. This guidance led her to a career in nursing and opened the door for her by providing a friend who just happened to be from a wealthy family—a family who had set up a scholarship fund for people just like Judith who desired to better their lives through education. The fascinating aspect of Judith's story was she met this friend in the most unexpected place—an elevator! They got stuck in one for an hour and ended up becoming friends through the experience!

"During my last week in the hospital, Judith came into my room one day and said not a word. She just walked over to my bed, laid a book beside me, then turned around and walked out. I thought it was very bizarre that she didn't say anything and started to become offended. I picked up the book she had left and looked at the cover. The title of the book was *The Godtown Guideline Handbook*. I thought, "What the hell is this?" I opened it up and on the first page there was one word written in small print. It said, "listen."

"Well, by this point, I was pretty open to anything, so I listened. It sounds simple, doesn't it? Please remember I'd been flat on my back for four months and had been an audience to Judith's words for just as long, so I was well prepared to listen. I just didn't quite know how to do it. Fortunately, my mind was somewhat clear because it was not cluttered with substance abuse, and I heard my inner voice within minutes of Judith's exit from my room.

"I was overwhelmed with the beauty of my conversations with my inner voice. There again, I was able to focus on them because I didn't have much else to focus on. I spent that last week in the hospital filling up my handbook with hours and hours of holy communication and prayer. I had never felt so alive! I had never felt so loved! It was a miracle. Judith had been my angel of light and I loved her dearly.

"The day finally came for my release. This was a big media event, and I was ready. The label capitalized on it by having Tommy, Claude, and Jesse wheel me out of the hospital. Actually, they would have been there for me anyway without encouragement from the suits, but I didn't mind a little media manipulation. They certainly didn't mind the extra hype, either. You never can have enough publicity, and free publicity is the best kind!"

By this time, I was totally lost in Steve's story. I'd crawled into it and felt like I'd been there experiencing every second of it right along with him. When he stopped talking, I was jolted out of my fantasy world and taken aback for a moment. I cleared my throat and said, "Wow!" (I know, I know, expand the vocabulary!) "Steve, I'm so amazed by what you've just shared with me. You're confirming my own experience and I'm so grateful for your honesty."

Steve replied, "Well, Desmond, the best part is still to come. You see, when the boys wheeled me out of the hospital, there were hundreds of people waiting for me. True, some were from the media, but there were also hundreds of fans, complete with signs and banners. I started to cry, I was so touched by the scene. I looked to my right and there was Judith, front and center. I smiled at her and she waved to me. Then I looked to her left, and there stood the most exquisite woman I'd ever seen. She was beautiful to me and had the same glow Judith possessed. I made the guys stop pushing me, then motioned for Judith to come over. She stepped around the hospital administrator and knelt by my side. I asked her if she knew the young lass who had been standing beside her. She looked over to where she had been and asked if I was referring to the brunette woman who was wearing the beige skirt. I said, yes, that was the one. A smile lit up Judith's face, and she answered that she did know her. Then she didn't say anything else. I waited for her to continue, but she just kept staring at me with a knowing look. I finally said in exasperation, "Judith, who is she?"

Judith answered, "She's my daughter, Steve. Her name is Katherine. Would you like to meet her?" She got up, went over and fetched her daughter. Now, keep in mind, everyone there was watching this happen, so hundreds and hundreds of eyes were upon us. I was unaware of all of them. At that moment, I was only seeing one person. When Judith returned, she announced, 'Steve Barham, please meet my daughter, Katherine.'

"Katherine extended her hand and said, 'Hello, Steve. It's very nice to meet you.' My heart stopped! Her touch sent chills through my body. I knew at that very moment I'd met the woman I was going to spend the rest of my life with. And I have. Katherine and I have been married for nineteen years. She is still the most beautiful woman I have ever seen. I am madly in love with her. She is a gift from God, as is her mother...and so is the healing experience I had in the hospital. Everything's connected. What I thought was going to be the most devastating experience of my life turned into the most exquisite blessing I've ever had!"

When he finished, I was crying. I could've felt a little silly, but didn't. I knew he'd understand, and when I looked at him, I noticed he had tears in his eyes, also.

This man deeply loved his wife. I'd seen a picture of the two of them in the magazine I mentioned earlier, and at the time I thought Katherine was an attractive woman but no beauty. In fact, I remember being surprised at how plain she appeared. Of course, I was so into image and my own perception of physical perfection, it doesn't surprise me that I'd overlooked her loveliness. I realized through this story the wonder of God-given love. Steve and Katherine had been blessed with it. They had both allowed God to guide them to each other.

I focused my attention on Steve again and decided to ask a very important question. I'd consistently asked my inner voice about Godtown but had been told to continue going through the process of "living in love" each day and I'd discover it. I'd tried to talk God into telling me where it was but had been told I should be of "no worry" about finding it. It dawned on me that I could feel comfortable asking Steve about this because he'd lived for many years in the arms of love and might give me some insight.

I took a deep breath and said, "You mentioned Humanville quite a few times during your story. You also talked about the *Godtown Guideline Handbook.* Can you tell me what Godtown is? I wasn't certain it existed until recently, but now think I can eventually get to it. I just don't know exactly where it is. I don't think it's a suburb of Humanville but am not really sure. Do you know?"

He looked at me with warm eyes and said, "Desmond, tell you what. I would like for you to come to our home for dinner tomorrow night. I really want you to meet Katherine, and I promise you we will answer your question then. Is it possible you might be free?"

"Absolutely, Steve. I'd be thrilled to have dinner with you and your family tomorrow night. Thank you." I exclaimed.

He replied, "Oh, we'll be delighted to have you. You may bring a date, if you'd like to. Or come alone, it's up to you."

I said, "Well, if I can scrounge up an escort, I'll let you know by tomorrow noon. I don't want to leave you hanging, ok? Also, can I bring anything?"

Steve smiled. "Just yourself. We'll supply everything else. This will be lovely. I'm excited you can join us."

I thanked him again, then looked at my watch and asked if he needed to get back to the studio. He said that yes, it was probably about time to, so we departed the coffee shop and drove back to Magnolia.

When he got out of my car, he hesitated for a second then said, "Desmond, I'm very happy you are going to be a part of my album. I'll nail down a day for you to come in and lay your vocal down, but I need to figure out when we can work it in, first. If you'd be so kind to indulge me, I'll try to have a specific time for you by tomorrow night. Oh, you will need directions. Let me give you our home number. You can get them tomorrow when you call to confirm your date status, how's that?"

I told him that would be fine, so he jotted down their number. He winked as he got out of the car and said, "See you tomorrow night!" then turned, and with a spring in his step, walked back into the studio.

What an experience! He was, by far, the most intriguing person I'd ever met. Ok, maybe I've known other fascinating people, but he was certainly the most genuine and brilliant. I couldn't wait until the next evening!

WELCOME TO GODTOWN

I contemplated bringing a date to Steve and Katherine's home, but in the end decided against it. I really wasn't seeing anybody special and didn't think I was ready to ask Mark Henderson to a social gathering quite yet. He was nice and we'd been on a few more dates since our first dinner, but I suspected he might not understand any talk having to do with "Godtown" or an "inner voice." We'd been out a few nights before and he'd been a little demeaning to me during a discussion about his business. (He was a stockbroker.) We were talking about good investments based on the current market and I made a comment about one that seemed impressive. He snapped back and insinuated I couldn't understand finance because I was in the music industry instead of a "real career." He didn't know my educational background, which includes a Bachelor of Science with a minor in business, and graduate studies in Business Administration.

Instead of taking offense, I was able to recognize an insecurity in him that made him react to me in a belittling way. He was uncomfortable because he'd dated a singer once before (which he mentioned on our first date) and had felt awkward around her friends and work environment. His reaction really had nothing to do with me but with his feelings concerning an industry he was somewhat intimidated by.

Oh, if he only knew the truth! Since we work in this high-profile field, we think everybody in the world wants to work in it, also. We are extremely self-absorbed and absolutely wrong about this. The reality is most of the public does appreciate having music in their lives but have much greater things to focus on than figuring out what their next CD purchase will be. We provide atmosphere and entertainment. This does hold an element of importance, but it certainly doesn't rank up there with brain surgery and raising children, etc. I find it humorous that we put ourselves in such high regard within society, because most of us are actually running around petrified of not getting re-signed or getting fired because someone younger better understands the marketplace, or whatever. There is very little job security on either side of Humanville's music industry!

Anyway, my point is that I recognized the motivation for Mark's comments and didn't take them personally, which was a miracle, really. In the past I would've been upset by his words and would've questioned myself. I was able to continue the conversation without going to a defensive place. In fact, my response was objective, basically telling him any information he could provide to expand my knowledge on the subject was appreciated. It diffused his insecurity, so he felt comfortable the rest of the evening. Love really does work. You see, I didn't demean myself to boost Mark's self-worth. I could've agreed with him, but then I would not have shown self-love. I would have exhibited my own insecurity, and then this strange imbalance of power would've happened, and it could've gotten out of hand very quickly... you know, he shows his insecurity, I show mine, he shows more of his, etc. Truly a waste of energy. It's much easier to go to love first. The challenge is, like I've mentioned before, going there immediately instead of allowing fear to intercede and control our responses.

Ok, I'm getting off on a tangent here. Back to my decision not to bring a date to the Barham's home. I actually did call Julie and ask if she was free to go with me, but unfortunately she'd made previous plans that she couldn't get out of. She was very excited that I'd met Steve Barham and was disappointed she couldn't go but was extremely supportive. She also said she'd been doing terrific, trusted her inner voice on a consistent basis now and was receiving blessing after blessing. We'd decided to get together for dinner the next night to fill each other in on everything.

So, flying solo it was! I didn't mind. I called and left a message for the Barhams about my escort status, and Katherine called back later in the morning and left directions to their home. I was sorry I missed her call but was excited about meeting her. She sounded extremely nice on her message.

That evening, I reached their home around 7:30. Turning into the driveway, I noticed the house was beautiful but surprisingly understated. It sat on well-manicured grounds and was a large home, but I guess I expected somebody of Steve's stature to live in a castle. I mean, it was no secret he'd made a fortune through his producing credits, but what was more impressive was the fact he'd written or co-written almost every song Mammoth had ever cut. He didn't mention that aspect of his resume when we'd gone for coffee, but his writing success was common knowledge, so maybe he didn't feel he had to. Or he was humble about it. The truth is, he'd made some amazing business decisions early on in his career and had owned his own publishing for over eighteen years.

(This means he completely owned all the copyright on his publishing catalog. Let me explain. Instead of going to a publisher and giving up the ownership of his songs in return for advance money and draws, he had kept the control of his music. I know it's a little confusing, but song ownership is one of the most lucrative aspects of the music industry. You see, one song on an album can bring in approximately $80,000 to $100,000 per million copies sold. Now, if the song becomes a single—is played on radio— the performance money can reach up to $1,000,000 or more if it's a huge hit. Mammoth probably averaged three to five hits per album and sold an average of five million copies per album. They made twenty-one of them...one of which sold an amazing fifteen million copies! Steve wrote or co-wrote every single Mammoth song ever played on radio. Add the producing credits, plus all the other work he'd done over the years with other artists. You do the math! See what I mean? His worth had to be in the hundreds of millions of dollars. Ok, enough music 101.)

I parked my car in the driveway, got out and walked up to the front door. I had stopped and purchased a nice bottle of Merlot to give them, but while ringing the bell, I realized that I didn't know if they drank wine. It was too late to worry about that now. I was a little nervous, so quickly checked in with my inner voice. God was right there, as always. I asked for help to calm my nerves and was told in a very loving way, "Desmond, each moment you live in love is a blessing. You are about to walk into a house built on love, so embrace the spirit and return the spirit. There is no need for fear. You are not going to be judged, nor should you judge. Remember to walk in the light of giving and service, and your light will be reflected back to you tenfold. Have a wonderful time with newfound friends."

I was about to respond to God when the door to the house opened and there stood Katherine Barham. She was one of the most attractive women I'd ever seen! She was not classically beautiful but possessed the most amazing warmth and glow. Her skin was luminous and her dark hair was thick and luxurious. She was slim—not thin, about my height, and carried herself with a dancer's grace. She was elegant…yes that was it, she was extremely poised and elegant. I was a little spellbound, for when she said, "Oh, you must be Desmond. I'm Katherine Barham. Please come in!" all I could do is nod my head. I stepped forward and she took my arm and escorted me into the foyer.

Finally finding my voice, I responded, "Hello, Katherine. It's very nice to meet you. Oh, I brought you and Steve a bottle of wine," and clumsily handed her the bottle. Then added almost apologetically, "I didn't know if you drank wine, but hopefully if you do you like Merlot."

Katherine said, "Desmond, how kind of you! I assure you we are huge fans of the fermented grape, and your choice is superb. Thank you very much. Please, let me take your wrap."

She took my jacket and disappeared for a brief second to hang it in the coat closet. When she returned, I'd gained my composure enough to compliment their beautiful home.

"Oh," she remarked, "That's very sweet of you. Steve and I purchased this house two years ago and have been trying to fix it up ever since. It's slowly whipping into shape. Come, let me give you the grand tour, if you call a two minute walk-about a tour!"

I said, "Absolutely, I'd love to!" and with that, Katherine took my hand in hers and whisked me off on a quick jaunt around the house. It was actually exquisite on the inside. Every detail was beautiful. The moldings, rugs, antiques, etc. were breathtaking. It was fun to hear all the little stories she told about how they'd acquired the different pieces of art and furniture. I was totally enchanted.

After the tour, Katherine escorted me down the stairs to the "great room," as she called it. This was where the rest of the dinner party had gathered. I reached the doorway to the room and abruptly halted. There stood Steve, and next to him was Jacob Richards, the biggest young alternative rock artist in the world. He was a phenomenon! He had hit the scene three years before with a first album that had been so brilliant it had sold a staggering eleven million copies. His second album had sold two million more than his first. I mean, he was a musical genius! The thing that set him apart from his peers was the lyrical content of his music. He wrote all of his own material, and his songs were so powerful that they cut to the core of one's soul. His melodies were hypnotizing, like nothing anyone had ever heard before. I was a huge fan! I suddenly remembered Steve was Jacob's producer, so that explained why he was close to the Barhams.

There was also another couple standing with Steve and Jacob. I didn't recognize either the man or the woman, and next to them stood two young girls, teenagers, who I assumed were Steve and Katherine's daughters.

Everyone turned their attention toward us when we entered the room. Katherine made a subtle gesture with her arm and introduced me to the group as if I was a princess. Quite honestly, at that very moment, I felt like a princess. It was like stepping into a fairytale and being touched by a magic wand. You're probably thinking I said that because of the magnitude of my surroundings and the stature of the people I was with, but that wasn't it. Truthfully, there was a special energy. I can't explain it, really, but the room was filled with euphoric light. No, that explanation doesn't even properly honor it. There was a sense of home, which was puzzling, though, because I didn't know these people.

I stepped down two stairs into the room. Steve came over to me, kissed each side of my cheeks and proceeded to introduce me to the man and woman who I didn't know. Charles and Barbara Butler were old friends of the Barhams. He was a building contractor and his wife was an elementary school teacher. I introduced myself and they both shook my hand. They

were extremely nice and, as you might guess, had the "glow." Then Steve
introduced his daughters to me. The older girl was named Lily. She was
sixteen and absolutely adorable. Rose, at thirteen, was her younger sister.
She was more like her mother, stately and poised. They were both bundles
of joy and light. It was wonderful to meet them, and I mentioned I thought
their names were cool. They smiled and Katherine interjected by saying the
girls had picked out their own names by choosing when they "arrived on the
scene." I didn't understand, so Rose jumped in to explain that right before
each of them had been born, Katherine had received a bouquet of flowers
from a dear family friend. The first one contained beautiful lilies and as
soon as she smelled their fragrance, she went into labor. Lily was born ten
hours later. Then the same thing happened with the next pregnancy. A
bouquet of roses was delivered to the house (from the same friend).
Katherine smelled the flowers and immediately went into labor. Seven hours
later, Rose entered the world. I thought this was a fabulous story and said
so. I decided to tell how I was named and everyone thought it was hilarious.
The ice was broken!

After my story, Steve apologetically said he'd failed to introduce the other
guest in the room. He motioned toward Jacob Richards and stated Jacob
was a surrogate son. When I extended my hand, Jacob actually bypassed it
and hugged me! I wasn't expecting that, so was thrown off for a second. He
was still hugging me as he said that it was great to meet me, and I laughed as
I responded that the pleasure was all mine. As you might suspect, Jacob had
the same intense glow as the rest of the dinner party, so there was definitely
a theme here. He had a youthful, almost elfish energy, but at the same time
he was very cool and extremely likable. He finally let me go, and when I

stepped back, saw that he couldn't have been over twenty or twenty-one. He was just as adorable as the girls were, in his own way.

Katherine explained there was one guest who had called to say that he was going to be late but had encouraged everyone to proceed with appetizers. He'd be here shortly and she'd promised him we'd go ahead and nibble on some morsels until he arrived. With that, she asked all of us to move into the den area where some appetizers had been set out for us. I walked beside the girls, who, for some reason, seemed to be enthralled with me. (I've always had a bond with young people. I think it's because of a quality I emit that comes across as being a peer instead of an adult. At least that's what I've been told. I obviously had chosen not to bear children up to this point in life, and you probably think it's because I was so career-driven. The truth is, I'd been so lost in anorexia and bulimia that I couldn't imagine bringing a child into the nightmare of my disease. I also had a body image distortion and was petrified of the changes that happen during pregnancy. I had cried many a night because I really did desire to be a mother, but thought I'd never be blessed with the freedom from my disease to be given this miracle. I briefly wondered if this dream could be achieved, now. I prayed I'd find out someday.)

The girls were impressed with my outfit. It wasn't really anything special, but I'd found it in the junior department of a very cool store in the city. I looked more like a teenager than a grown woman. I didn't mean to do this. I'd just been aware of how I'd overdone it the day I'd met Steve for coffee, and didn't want to be so extreme at dinner. (*Still* worried about the image thing…although, proper attire is always a challenge, isn't it!?!)

We made our way into the den. As I proceeded to the couch, my eyes glanced at a plaque hanging over the fireplace. I looked casually at first and then did a double take. I didn't want to look shocked or draw attention to myself, but I couldn't believe what it said! Luckily, everyone was talking to each other and didn't notice my reaction, so I silently slid over to the fireplace and set my drink on the mantel. This gave me an opportunity to get close to the plaque. I stared at it and read the inscription over and over again. I held back tears as a flood of emotion came rushing from my heart because, there... in front of me, were the words, "Welcome to Godtown."

I had to force my eyes off the wall and when I glanced around the room, Steve was looking at me, smiling. I peered back at him with a questioning face, and he casually made his way over to me. When he reached me, he placed his hand on my shoulder and said, "Are you confused, Desmond?" I just shook my head yes and he gave a small chuckle, "I understand. Come, take a walk."

I did as told, following him out the french doors onto the back deck. It was a wonderful evening, and the sky was full of stars. It was just warm enough to be comfortable for a few minutes without a jacket. He led me down a path to the garden area. We stopped in front of a beautiful pond that had a fountain in the middle. It was lit up with multi-colored lights.

I turned to him and asked, "Steve, what's going on?"

In a very gentle tone, he replied, "Desmond, Katherine and I have lived in Godtown for our entire marriage. We were brought together by the power of

God and through the guidance of our inner voices. We've tried to live our lives with love as our foundation and have raised our children through God's direction."

I replied, "I don't understand. Where is Godtown?"

Steve smiled, placed his hand over his heart, and said, "It's right here."

I looked down to where his hand was resting on his chest, then lifted my eyes to meet his. I didn't respond, so he nodded his head and continued. "Godtown is where we reside once we accept the fact that God lives in us and we acknowledge our inner guidance. When we finally learn to listen and trust our inner voice, which is the voice of God, we perceive every aspect of life through the eyes of love, not fear. You already know this, so you shouldn't be surprised at these words."

I agreed with him that, yes, I had learned this from my inner voice.

He carried on. "So, you see, once we integrate with God and trust love, we interact with the world in an entirely different manner. We recognize that we have the most powerful force in the universe leading our way through the path of life. Love is our light, our guide, our strength, and our protector."

I said, "I do understand what you're telling me about love and God, but I thought Godtown was a real community…where people lived in harmony, joy, and happiness. I envisioned streets of gold, I guess, and beauty everywhere and, I don't know, a castle maybe. I thought it was a tangible town. This is Humanville…"

Steve smiled even broader and said, "Godtown is all of those things and more. It's a very real place. The thing you don't grasp is the fact that you can choose to live in Godtown, or you can remain in Humanville. Godtown is the home you create when you choose to see everything through love and not fear. It is glorious and you have the power to create it in your own life."

I kept listening to him and slowly accepted what he was telling me. I have to admit, I'd made up a fantasy about Godtown and had thought it was almost impossible to reach. The idea it was accessible and that I was actually living there was amazing to me. I mean, my voice had assured me that I'd find it if I continued the daily process of living through love, but this was a total surprise. I was there, living in Godtown!

All of a sudden, this wave of joy rushed through me. I laughed out loud and Steve recognized at once that I'd finally understood what he was telling me. I threw my arms up in the air, looked at the stars, and cried, "Thank you!!" then looked at Steve, and he opened his arms and hugged me. I hugged him back, then stepped back and wiped a few tears from my eyes. I finally said, "You and your family were sent to me by God, weren't you?"

He responded, "Yes, we were. We pray to be of service and ask God to lead us to those who are looking for Godtown. We've been blessed with many new friends over the years, and we love them all with the love we have within us. As you probably noticed, everyone here tonight is a part of Godtown."

"Yes, I did notice. Everyone has the most beautiful glow, and they emit a light that has embraced me," I replied.

"Well, you're also in the light and are glowing, too. You're a part of this community. Welcome to Godtown!"

I thanked him for his words and he smiled and nodded, then suggested we go back inside. As we walked into the house, I observed that everyone else was carrying on and didn't seem to notice that we'd left the room for a moment. When we joined the others, the last guest had finally arrived. His back was to us, so he didn't see us approach him.

Steve said loudly enough for the entire room to hear, "Well, it's about time you showed up!" His voice caught everyone's attention, so all eyes looked our direction. At that moment, the man he was talking to turned around, and I actually gasped. Steve rushed ahead of me and went over to hug him.

He said, "Well, old boy, we thought for a moment you were not going to grace us with your company!"

The man hugged Steve back and exclaimed, "Hey, don't give me a hard time. You know I was doing you a favor. Katherine would not have let me in this house if I'd shown up without her special dessert. If I remember correctly, *you* were the one who called and asked me to pick it up on my way over!"

Steve stepped back from the embrace and laughed. "Ok, ok, you got me. I can't pull one over on you anymore. You've gone and grown up on me! "

Steve turned his attention to me and said, "When we were kids, I could get him to do anything I wanted and he never argued back. I had him tricked into believing I knew everything. Guess the facade is over! Desmond, I'd like to introduce my baby brother, Jonathan."

Jonathan left his brother's side and walked over to me. He extended his hand and said, "Hello, Desmond. It's an honor to meet you."

I was tongue-tied! I'd never seen a more attractive man. He was about 6'1", olive-skinned, and muscular. His hair was light brown, and he had the clearest, most piercing-blue eyes I'd ever seen. On top of everything else, he carried himself with a casual elegance that made him very approachable. I opened my mouth to speak, but nothing came out. I quickly smiled to cover up my lack of voice, finally recovering enough to say, "Hello, Jonathan. Yes." Ok, that didn't come out the way I'd intended. I just couldn't form any more words. I stood there, staring, and he squeezed my hand before releasing it, and asked, "Ok, you two, where have you been hiding this lovely creature?"

Katherine laughed and said that Steve had prayed for me and all of a sudden I came out of nowhere to help him with his album. Although apparently this was true, I still blushed and wasn't sure how to respond to all the attention. I was acting like a teenager! This was silly, I'd met many handsome men before and had rarely been at a loss for words. Luckily, Rose spoke up and broke the spell I was in. She said, "Uncle Jonathan, did you remember to bring the surprise you promised me?"

Jonathan turned to Rose and grinned, saying, "As a matter of fact, I did. It's actually waiting for you in the foyer." With that, Rose shot out of the room and, for a brief moment, left poise and grace behind and became a normal thirteen-year-old. It was cute to see her be a kid for a minute.

Jonathan turned back to me and quipped, "I warned Steve and Katherine I was bringing Rose her belated birthday present but failed to tell them what it was." Steve overheard Jonathan and was about to ask what he'd brought for Rose, when she came running back into the den, squealing with delight. In her arms was an eight-week old puppy. She was overjoyed, and it kept licking her face and wiggling with so much energy that she almost dropped it three times.

Everyone "oohhed and awwwed" over the dog, and Steve just laughed out loud and said, "Ok, now you've done it! Katherine and I hold you fully responsible for the future ruined carpet and furniture! Just thought we'd let you know now, so you could prepare yourself for all of our belly-aching."

Katherine ran over to Rose and asked her daughter if she could hold her new "baby" for a minute. Rose gave the puppy to her mother, and it proceeded to lick Katherine's face with the same enthusiasm it had shown to Rose.

Everyone laughed at the sight of Katherine's drenching, and when she finally couldn't take anymore, gave the bundle back to Rose.

Jonathan enjoyed watching his present create such excitement. I almost felt like an intruder in this close-knit family, but these people embraced life. They loved sharing their joy with others, and I sensed that, so I was honored to be a witness to such a display of love.

Katherine excused herself to wash her hands. When she returned, she announced that we could all head to the dining room, because dinner was ready to be served. She looked over at Rose and told her that she could come later if she wanted to play with her new gift a little longer. Rose squealed with delight again. Katherine took that as an "Ok mum," left it at that, turned, and led us all into the dining room.

I was having a great time. It was just so much fun to be around truly happy people! I was awe-struck with the Godtown realization, but my joy extended into the acknowledgment that this happiness could be created inside me. My thoughts drifted for a second. I could extend this level of joy to everyone I came into contact with. What a gift it was to help others feel happy just because I was happy...and I was happy. Really happy, and I knew my voice was right with me, enjoying the evening as much as I was. God was a part of me and I was a part of God. We were one with each other and with everyone in the room.

I came out of my daydream just in time to be seated at the dining table. It was beautifully set, but once again, in an understated way. I was asked to sit wherever I liked, so just placed myself in the chair closest to me. Jonathan sat next to me (which made me more happy—must be developing a little crush!), and everyone else took seats around us.

We had a lovely dinner, shared stories and laughter, and all too soon the evening came to an end. I thanked Katherine and Steve for an amazing night and they both said it had been their pleasure. I told Charles and Barbara I'd really enjoyed getting to know them and expressed the same sentiment to Jacob. I added that I was looking forward to hearing the new album, which he and Steve had just finished. He promised to get me a copy as soon as the artwork for the cover was complete. Then I went over and hugged the girls, expressing to them how much fun I'd had. They returned the hug and made me promise to go shopping with them. I laughed and said we'd try to work that out.

Jonathan offered to escort me out, so Katherine fetched my jacket and I bid my last farewells, then walked outside with him. When we got to my car, he told me he'd enjoyed meeting me and I returned the compliment. We stood there in an awkward silence for a moment then both tried to speak at the same time, which made us laugh. As he started to say something else, Steve came flying out the front door and yelled, "Oh, Desmond, I'm so glad you haven't departed yet. I forgot to tell you I'd like to record your vocal the day after tomorrow, if you can make it."

I said, "Of course, Steve, that sounds great. What time would you like me to be at the studio?"

He answered, "I should have everything up and ready to go by eleven. Is that too early for you to sing?"

I said, "No, that will be fine."

"Perfect" he exclaimed. "See you then."

I didn't want to be rude, but secretly hoped he would say good-bye and go back in the house, so Jonathan could finish saying what he'd started to tell me. However, Steve didn't move. He just stood there with a big grin on his face and his arm around his brother. It was so endearing that I had to smile myself and decided not to wait it out. It was obvious he didn't know he'd interrupted anything. I said goodnight to both of them and Jonathan opened my car door. I got in, waved bye, then drove away as I watched their reflections wave back at me in the rearview mirror...

I ALREADY LIVE HERE!?!

As soon as I drove out of eyesight of the Barham house, I asked my inner voice to talk to me. As always, God was right there, waiting.

Me: Ok... you didn't tell me about Godtown... you said to follow my daily process of living through love...why didn't you just let me know what was going on?

God: Desmond, if I had told you that you were already living in Godtown, you would not have understood where Godtown truly is. Tonight you had the opportunity to experience a home environment where love is the foundation. It made a big impact on you.

Me: Well, I have to agree with you. It's just, I've been searching for Godtown for a very long time. If I'd known the truth about it, I would've accepted and embraced it immediately.

God: Oh, but you would not have. It would have felt anti-climatic to you if I had shortened your journey by telling you that you had already arrived. It would have seemed too easy and simple, after all of your searching, to find out you carried Godtown within you. By observing the life of someone you admire, you had the opportunity to understand and respect it, because you respect Steve and his family. You enjoyed your evening, yes?

Me: Oh, very much! Thank you for blessing me with tonight. It was life-changing!

God: Every moment lived through love is life-changing. Rest assured you can have as much joy in your life every day as you did this evening. You see, living in Godtown is very simple. You just choose love, every day. That is all it takes to have a wonderful, happy life.

I knew this was right. It was up to me...I had the power to be positive or to be negative and was responsible for that choice.

I mentioned this and God replied, "Yes, you can perceive every second of the life you live through either love or fear, you pick."

Me: In other words, I can choose to reside in Godtown or can remain in Humanville.

God: Exactly.

Me: So the two co-exist within each other? How could I have not seen Godtown before now if it's such a real place?

God: You wore a mask of fear that prevented you from seeing and recognizing love. There have been many times during your life you have interacted with Godtown residents, but your perception of these people caused you to not trust their sincerity. You viewed everyone through guarded eyes. You judged others' motivations based on negative interpretation. Remember the time your mother took time off from her work to help you when you were so busy with all your extra-curricular activities? This was during your last year in high school. She thought you would be so overwhelmed with responsibility you would need her help and support. You assumed she was trying to be around you because she didn't trust you and wanted to control you and your actions. You judged her very harshly and could not see the love, support, and service she was trying to bestow upon you. You were living in Humanville, and your mother was a part of Godtown.

Me: Whoa, now wait a minute, God. My mother had her share of issues that she dealt with and I was conditioned to respond to her in a certain way because of past experience. Why didn't my mother ever explain Godtown to me if she was aware of it?

God: Desmond, I told you that you can choose to reside in Godtown or live in Humanville. This is a daily decision. Just because you have discovered where Godtown is, it does not mean you will automatically wake up every morning and reside in it. You could live in Godtown one day, then fall back into a place of fear and be in Humanville the next. Once you are aware you have a choice, it seems logical you would always desire light instead of dark, but there will still be times you battle with this decision.

Your mother was no different than you. She had so much love for you inside her heart. When she was not afraid, her light was very bright. There were times, though, she fell into the dark. She struggled to remain positive, but was insecure and did not feel worthy of love, either. You could not recognize her need for nurturing because of your own darkness. You lived in a tunnel and could not get out because you stubbornly wanted to control your environment. You thought you were "protecting your turf," but what you were really doing was building a prison for yourself. You became anorexic to exert power over your parents and display control over your own life. It didn't work, did it? You were angry and she knew it. Your mother vacillated between Godtown and Humanville because she allowed herself to fall into the trap of re-acting instead of consistently acting out of love. You see, if you are nervous about being judged by a fear-based person, you start acting out of fear, also. You try to read and anticipate the moods of this person and lose your love-based center. You also become insecure because you have no grounding, no foundation. You have the right to stand strong in love and when you have the confidence to do so, fear has no power. When you see this person through loving eyes, it is easy to understand his or her actions. Your mother did not share Godtown with you because she did not have the confidence to live there long enough to teach you about it. This was a challenge in her life. She struggled with self-worth in much the same way you have.

Me: She did? I would never wish my struggle on anyone—especially my mother. I didn't know any of this. So, there were times she was totally sincere and I shut her down? How could I have been so cruel and not seen her pain?

God: Desmond, she was your parent. Children have a difficult time seeing parents objectively. It was not your responsibility to take care of your mother's emotional and spiritual life, for she could have come to Me in times of fear. You developed a strained relationship because you both had similar strengths and weaknesses. You learned yours from her and she learned hers from her upbringing. It is so important to understand the impact parental guidance has on a child. If you teach a child to fear, the child will fear. If you teach a child to love, the child will love. A child raised in Humanville will not believe he or she is love-worthy. A child raised in Godtown will know he or she is worthy of complete love and will also extend love to everyone and everything in life. Every human is born completely connected to Me and to love. Fear is learned.

I agreed with what God was saying and thought about the times I'd misunderstood my mother because of my own insecurities. I couldn't see how much pain she was in. I asked if there was anything I could do to let her know that I finally understood her heart.

God : Yes, there are two things. First, you can thank her for giving you life by telling her you love her completely and unconditionally. Secondly, you can pray for love to be the source of her strength and guidance.

I promised to do both immediately. I wanted to go back to the part of the conversation that talked about how I had developed a prison for myself...

Me: God, how did I get out of the anorexic prison? I didn't choose to leave the disease, there were just some circumstances that kind of stopped my ability to push myself so hard.

God: Do you remember an elderly man who you befriended when you were in college?

Me: Oh, yeah, sure I remember. He was always sitting at the same table in the student union cafeteria every time I went in after class to get a cup of coffee. I used to sit down next to him and he'd talk to me. He was such a gracious, interesting man. We became friends... wait a minute, now that I think about it, he had a glow—I was very attracted to his energy.

God: Exactly. This man lived in Godtown. He was one of many people you interacted with during your struggle with anorexia who lived through Me. He prayed for you every day. So did many, many others who were aware of your pain and struggle.

Me: How did they know about my disease? I didn't even know about anorexia during this time. I thought I was just an over-achiever. I mean, maybe I was in denial, but was it that obvious to other people?

God: Oh, yes. You were in grave danger and it was very apparent to those around you that you were in the grips of a serious struggle.

Me: God, I didn't know any of this...it's scary. I tricked myself into believing no one could tell what I was hiding.

I shook my head in sorrow. I wasn't fooling anyone, except me. Good grief, how did I lose myself for all those years? I couldn't bring back the lost time... I decided to not dwell on that fact for the moment. It was too sad a thought. Instead, I asked about prayer...

Me: All right, I have a question. You've told me I have the free will to either open my heart to let prayer in or ignore it. It doesn't go away, but it's not effective if I don't let it in, is it?

God: Loving prayer is always effective because it will never leave you. It was waiting for you and subtly reminded you it was there. Remember My explanation about how prayer works? It remains in your "unopened mail" box and beeps periodically to let you know that it's waiting for you. Once again, I do not wish to bring the holy process of prayer down to a comparison to a computer system, but for the sake of clarity, I will use the example again to illustrate how you received your prayers. Your heart did open a little every time you conversed with your elderly friend. He gave you a sense of encouragement and hope because he always told you that you could reach your dreams. He had been a successful professor at one point and had overcome his own struggles to succeed. His personal stories warmed your heart and you received a little of his love because you felt safe with him. Do you remember?

Me: I do remember. He made me feel good about myself. For a brief moment after talking with him, I'd have hope. It would leave very quickly, but at least it would be there for a second. I used to go to the student union for no reason other than to find him. He always made my day brighter.

I'd reached my home by this point and was, once again, sitting in my car having this conversation. It was completely dark outside, so at least my neighbor couldn't see me. I decided to go inside because it was starting to get chilly. I got out and walked up to my house, still deep in thought. As I tried to unlock my front door, I dropped my keys. As usual, I'd forgotten to change the burned out light bulb on the front porch. I had to drop to my knees and feel around for the key ring and snagged my cool, way over-priced pants in the process. (That doesn't surprise you, does it?). I finally found them, unlocked the door, and walked in the house. This brief distraction prevented me from focusing on God's words for a minute. I decided to get some water and check my messages before continuing the conversation.

When I listened to my voice mail, there was a message from Julie con-firming dinner for the next evening and suggesting a restaurant where we could meet. Hearing her voice reminded me of her cousin, Shelly, who had died of anorexia. I decided to ask God about the circumstances surrounding Shelly's death, since it was closely associated to what we'd been talking about.

I got my water, sat down in my oversized cuddle chair, as I called it, and cleared my mind to continue...

Me: I think what you're telling me is that I was saved from anorexia because I received a lot of prayer from the people in my life who were concerned about me. My heart opened just a little for my elderly friend and this, in turn, allowed prayer to reach me. So love was able to intervene and help me get through anorexia. God, this makes sense, but I have a very important question. My friend Julie had a cousin named Shelly who died of anorexia. Why did she lose her battle? Julie said that the family surrounded Shelly and I'm sure she had prayers for her healing, also. How do you explain her death?

I thought God would stumble a little with this answer. Not that I didn't trust my voice, but I assumed the situations were similar enough that Shelly should have been healed, also. Love's wisdom, once again, gave me clarity.

God: Shelly was trapped in a fear far deeper than the darkness you experienced and it had complete power over her life. She couldn't find any hope. As I have told you, I deal with everyone individually, so every relationship is unique and special. Shelly is a gentle spirit, but as she fell deeper into darkness her soul became buried under layers and layers of fear.

I was confused , so I questioned this.

Me: God, help me understand. Shelly died because her fear wouldn't let her go. It appears she killed herself, really. I don't get what you are telling me.

God: Shelly's body became so weak and emaciated, it started literally destroying vital organs in its quest to find nourishment. Shelly was so lost in her fear that she allowed this to happen within her. I was there, waiting for her to acknowledge Me and ask for help, but her fear prevented this from happening. The time came for Shelly to be released from her body. She did choose this.

Death is not a punishment. As I have told you before, it is rebirth. Shelly's passing was painful because if she had chosen to live her life through love, she would have spent her time here experiencing joy and happiness. Her life was tormented with pain and sickness because she chose fear. As a result, she suffered greatly and never had the chance to know what a love-based existence really could feel like.

Me: Are you saying that Shelly would have died at the same age no matter what happened to her?

God: I am telling you that every human has a purpose to fulfill and lessons to be learned. Every decision you make will lead you to the next one. Each decision gives you the opportunity to choose love or fear. You design your path based on the decisions you make. Shelly chose to allow fear to have power over her body and heart. She chose to continue on this path and, as a result, every decision she made took her one step farther away from love. The further away she traveled, the harder it was for her to hear Me and follow love's guidance like you finally chose to do. Each of you has the power to create your own destiny based on these decisions.

Shelly learned a great lesson in love the day she died. She realized she chose her pain and suffering and ultimately chose her death.

Me: Will you tell me what her lesson was, God?

God: Desmond, Shelly's relationship with Me was, and is, a sacred one. Every relationship between Soul and Spirit is holy and personal. I will tell you that Shelly had the opportunity to finally experience unconditional love that day and her fear left her. I will ask you a question. How would you feel if you had been Shelly?

I paused for a moment and remembered when I was in the throws of anorexia, recalling the horrible nightmare of being trapped in my body and drowning in enormous fear. As uncomfortable as it was, I made myself think about what it would've been like if my body had finally given up. I actually started crying, knowing how very close I'd been at one point. I finally answered God's question.

Me: If I'd lost my battle with anorexia, I would've died at about the same age Shelly did. I can only guess, but standing in Your glory only magnifies the joy of love and the sadness of unnecessary suffering. I would've finally seen, in a very clear way, how much pain I'd thrown on my heart, mind, spirit, and body. I also would've seen how much torment I'd given my family and friends. I would've been extremely remorseful for my choices. I can only imagine what it's like to be released into Your light and to actually be born into the beauty of Your unconditional love. I think I would've been overwhelmed with the blessing of rebirth but would've regretted my decision to leave my life and body so soon. And I would've clearly seen that I'd possessed the power to heal all along but had not done so because of my fear. That would be a terrible realization because the outcome of my decisions would've already transpired. I'd finally understand the meaning of *consequence for choices*. The consequence of my decisions would be the missed opportunity for me to choose the path of love and happiness while I'd been alive. I'd recognize that I'd had the right to love myself all along and just hadn't done it. I would've regretted this so much! Oh God, is this what she went through the day she died?

God: It appears you do understand how Shelly felt. Rest assured she is very loved and is very happy now.

I stopped this interaction and sat in a daze. I could've easily been Shelly, and though I'd escaped her experience, I had almost died while lost in bulimia. I just sat there, not moving, as the last blinder came off and I saw, with complete clarity, the truth. I'd been given a miracle, a second chance, and God believed in me. I was loved, unconditionally. I'd been taught how to love and to be loved. My inner voice had healed me from disease and had helped me find a love for myself I didn't know I had a right to feel.

That moment, I gave my heart completely to God and decided to trust love's guidance, follow love's direction, and devote my life to being of service. Even though I'd believed the commitment had been there for the last couple of months, I hadn't even been close to experiencing the amazing love God was offering me. It finally clicked. I recognized that I may never have a husband, children, or a famous artist career, but I'd still be totally fulfilled because love was the center of my life. Following love's direction would complete me. I was never going to feel alone again because God was with me every second of every minute and would never leave me.

Suddenly, I realized something just as phenomenal. In turning my heart completely over to God, I was also turning my heart completely over to myself! I was empowering my soul, mind, heart, and spirit through God. We were one, as long as I lived in love and not fear.

I felt so strong and invincible! I was filled up with love's light, and knew I had the ability to integrate with my higher self (my voice, God) every second of every day. It was not only possible, but also extremely easy to do if I only chose to do so in every instance.

My last thought of the night was that I'd finally found my answer. It had been with me all along, and I truly understood. I knew with conviction that I'd become a citizen of Godtown and could remain here, forever. I was worthy of staying, worthy of love, and worthy of loving...

IT'S NOT OVER YET…

I bet you were thinking my story was at its end. Nope, not yet…close, though. You see, I fell asleep in my cuddle chair after finishing my talk with God and didn't move until the next morning. I awoke with such peace and happiness! I was floating, though should've been stiff, considering I'd slept in a contorted position for hours! On the contrary, I could take on the world. I immediately checked in and said good morning to my voice, had a moment of prayer, then got up and started the morning routine.

After coffee, I decided to call Julie back and confirm our dinner plans. She didn't pick up, so I left a message, then went and showered. I was singing and dancing around…baby, this was euphoria… I mean, I was literally break-dancing in there. Ok, maybe not break-dancing, but definitely grooving to my own beat. It was great!

I got cleaned up and dressed, then headed out to go do errands. Every time I went in somewhere, people responded to me with happiness and joy. I was having so much fun! There was even one older woman at the bank (standing in front of me in line) who actually hugged me by the time it was her turn to go to the window. I just started talking to her, made her laugh, and before long she was telling me about her grandchildren and showing me pictures, etc. Cool!

I was glowing. I could feel it. People were turning their heads when I entered a room, but it wasn't because they were attracted to me physically. They noticed "the glow" and were looking at me differently than when I'd tried to gain attention by having the perfect image. I can't quite explain it, but this was real, whereas before it had been manipulated.

That evening, I met Julie for dinner. We were like two schoolgirls giggling about our crushes, except that we were talking about God and love. Halfway through the meal, I noticed the couple sitting one table away from us was trying to overhear our conversation. I smiled, remembering the time I'd eavesdropped on the two people in the coffee shop. We were creating the same curiosity for this couple. I turned at one point and said hello. Julie did the same and we spoke briefly to them. Geez, this was so great! I said a silent little prayer as we turned back around and it dawned on me that I'd been given the same prayer the day I'd first heard about Godtown. My "glowing" people had sent love my way just as I was doing now. That's how it works! We're all connected. It was so much fun to actually understand the process.

Julie told me about what was going on in her life, and I shared mine with her. She was doing well and had found a real peace about so many things: her brother, her ex-husband, her future, etc. She was working constantly and had just completed a national commercial that was going to make her a great deal of money. She'd also met a man she was very interested in, as he was in her. His name was John and he'd noticed her one evening while she'd been attending a play. Apparently, he was a professor of psychology and had met her brother once before he'd died. They discovered this while chatting during intermission. John asked if she'd like to join him after the performance for a late snack and she felt comfortable accepting. They talked for hours the first night and she learned he lived in Godtown, also. It had grown from there. I was so happy for her. She said it was the first time she'd really opened her heart and trusted the process of love. She added that it was so easy to be in each other's lives. Things just flowed because they respected each other with such a sincere love. I actually clapped my hands when I heard this. Man, this love thing was an incredible way to live!

We ended our night with a hug and I told her I loved her. It was so funny, because this show of affection was *not* done in Humanville, but we weren't in Humanville, anymore. Everyone around us might've been, but we were in Godtown and didn't give a second thought to what others were thinking. What freedom we'd found!

I drove home and thought about the dinner. I remembered the couple we'd talked to and reminisced about the people I'd met that day in the coffee shop. I decided to ask about them...

Me: God, did those two people pray for me the day I met them?

God: Yes they did. That is why you were so intrigued with them. You felt the connection. They sent love and it washed over you. You have referred to it as a spark, but in actuality you were given an ocean of love that day. You needed an ocean to be sent to you. You had so much fear that you had an extremely thick raincoat on. Most of the love couldn't reach you, but you did let one drop in. Think of how powerful even one drop of love is. It changed your life, didn't it?

Me: Yes, it did. Did the people tonight receive my prayer?

God: Yes, but they will have to choose whether they will be open to it or not. Rest assured your prayer will stay with them and in time, hopefully, they will listen to love.

I thought about my journey (never came up with another word for "journey", did I?) and remembered the old woman who came to me in the park. Surprisingly, I'd never asked about her.

Me: Who was the woman in the park? How did she know who I was and why did she come to me?

God: You were reaching out to love and love found you. Think of her as an angel of light sent to you to help you find Me. She was led to you.

Me: An angel? Really? How cool! (Ok, did I know any other expressions than "really" and "how cool"? Oh, yeah, there was "wow" too...whew!) I wasn't sure about whether angels were real. Is that why she had an extra *Godtown Guideline Handbook* with her?

God: Angels are all around you, in every walk of life. Everyone who lives in Godtown is called upon to be an angel for those in need. You also are an angel. You were tonight for the people you talked to at dinner. Angels spread love and that's what you did. The woman you met in the park was a special angel sent to extend a healing hand to you. She gave you the handbook that had been given to her by another angel.

Me: But, God, the handbook had nothing written in it except "listen." How could it have been her handbook? Wouldn't it have been full of her conversations with you?

God: The *Godtown Guideline Handbook* is a tool that helps you get to the place of total integration with Me. There comes a time you don't need the handbook anymore because you and I become one. You realize you don't have to refer to it because you completely trust that every answer you need to live a love-based life is inside you and can be accessed through Me. It is at this point you become a citizen of Godtown and can pass the handbook to another soul who needs it. You are open to guidance and are led through Me to the person you are supposed to give the handbook to. Sometimes this is an immediate experience. Sometimes it is years before you are asked to pass the handbook along to another.

Each human has a unique relationship with Me and will have different lessons to learn. The foundation of love never falters or shifts. The process of learning about the power and holiness of love, however, is different for everyone, depending upon the life situation he or she is born into. So, every person's *Godtown Guideline Handbook* will have different stories and interactions in it. No two are the same.

Me: But, how do those conversations end up in the handbook to begin with? Also, how do they disappear when the handbook shifts ownership?

God: This is what is referred to as a miracle. Trust that the power and strength of miracles are beyond human understanding. They are very real and every soul is worthy of experiencing a miracle of love. You have been blessed with many miracles, though at times you have not recognized them.

Me: Well, I won't try to push you into explaining how miracles work, for I do believe it's beyond my understanding. I'm just extremely grateful to now know I can receive Your love in such a beautiful way. Thank you...

God: You are welcome. Recognize you are also thanking yourself right now, for we are one. You and I. You are of Me, and I am of You. Rejoice in this knowledge.

I was rejoicing. Actually was thrilled. I was free...I was loved...I was happy...I was strong...I was wise...because of love...because of God...

MAKING MUSIC...

The next day was the big recording session with Steve Barham. Surprisingly, I wasn't nervous, just extremely excited. I was at the studio at 11:00 a.m. sharp and, as usual, had to wait about forty-five minutes for the engineer to get everything completely set up. Steve was there, so we had a chance to chat before I sang for him. I thanked him again for the wonderful evening in his home and he told me I'd made quite an impression on everyone there. Of course I said, "Really?" (Ok, it was at this point that I made myself promise to look into a course for extended vocabulary!!!) I blushed at the compliment and was about to respond when the engineer interrupted us to say the studio was ready.

I followed Steve into the control room and he said he was going to play the track for me first, then explain what he wanted me to do. The engineer started the song. I'm telling you, this was the most beautiful piece of music I'd ever heard!!! I know I'm repeating myself, but it truly was from another world. I sat mesmerized, and let every note wash over me. It was definitely the same feeling I'd get every time I spoke to God. How could that be? I couldn't answer that question, so I just sat there and enjoyed it.

When the track was finished, Steve spoke up and asked for my opinion. I was speechless...which seemed to be happening a lot in my new life. He smiled in understanding and said I'd just answered the question. He thanked me for the unspoken compliment, then started to explain what he wanted me to do. He had a recorder with him (which is a wooden, flute-like instrument) and told me he wanted my voice to become another instrument in the song. I wouldn't be singing words but singing sounds. He played the part on the instrument, then sang the phonetic tone he wanted me to copy. It was haunting and beautiful. He said apologetically that he wasn't really a singer and knew it would sound better with my voice doing it than his, but hopefully I was getting an idea of what he needed.

Boy, was I getting an idea! This was going to be incredible. I couldn't believe I was here and was going to get to be a part of this creation. I answered yes, I understood what he wanted and proceeded to sing back to him what he'd just demonstrated. I was pretty close, and he was impressed with my recall. I'd missed a couple of notes, but he quickly showed me what needed to be added, then off I went into the studio.

I got my cans on, and...oh, sorry. I'm speaking "studio talk". Cans are headphones. I have no idea where that nickname came from. They don't resemble cans, they don't sound like cans...hey, you know what? Maybe that nickname came from when we were little kids and made homemade telephones out of cans and strings. Did you ever do that? You know, make a hole in the bottom of a can, then thread a piece of string through it and attach it to another can. You can then hear an amplified version of your voice when you talk into the can at the other end... Am I getting off on a tangent, here? Ok, yes I am, but I'll ask around to find out if I'm right about this and let you know!

Anyway, the engineer started the track and I jumped in and started singing the part. I looked through the glass at Steve and he seemed pleased. I got through half the song before he stopped me to give a little direction. He started the track again. I applied his ideas to my performance and made it through the entire song. He asked me to do it one more time, so I did. Then he asked me to come into the control room.

I came in and stood next to where Steve and the engineer were sitting. Steve looked at me and just shook his head up and down, silently saying "yes." That made me happy. I realized I'd performed well. He asked the engineer to rewind the track and play it for us.

Just before the music started to play, Jonathan walked through the control room door. This startled me, and I blushed again. He came over and gave me a hug, then patted his brother on the back while shaking hands with the engineer. He asked if he was too late. Steve informed him the performance was over, but that the playback was about to begin. Jonathan smiled and said "great" while pulling up a chair to sit down next to where I was standing.

I was nervous! Couldn't believe it. I was fine while singing, but a cute guy walks in and I'm jelly. All of a sudden, I became shy and wanted to crawl out of the room. I immediately recognized, though, that shyness was actually fear and that I had no reason to fear anything with Jonathan, or Steve for that matter. I said a little prayer to God, and my voice was right there with calming words. I relaxed just in time to hear the beginning of the song. It was magnificent! You really couldn't hear me, specifically, but my tonality cut through the track and added a dimension to the music that hadn't been there before. I was thrilled and could tell that Steve was, too. I looked down at Jonathan and he had his eyes closed, totally captured by the sound. It was such a sense of accomplishment and honor.

When the song finished, Steve looked at me and actually had tears in his eyes. I understood this was a completed dream for him. He thanked me profusely and I told him it had been my pleasure. He then asked the engineer to run it one more time and we all listened again. It was just as impressive the second time through. I couldn't have been more pleased.

After the session was over, Jonathan asked if I had plans for lunch. An immediate "no" was my answer, and he asked if I'd like to join him. You don't have to guess what I said. I blurted out "yes" before he even finished asking, which was a little embarrassing, but fortunately he just laughed and thought I was funny. He escorted me to his car and then drove to a quaint bistro in the canyon. I'd never been there but had heard a lot about it.

When we got seated, Jonathan complimented me again on the work I'd just done. My response was, "Thank you, but I can't take any credit. Steve just told me what to do and I did it."

Jonathan countered, "Yes, but your gift was the instrument. Your voice sounds beautiful on the song."

"Wow," I exclaimed. (Don't say it...extended vocabulary school!!!) "Well, to be honest with you, I thought so, too. My tonality did add a special dimension."

"Yeah, you're right." Jonathan said. "The board of directors is going to be so excited about how this album is turning out!"

I didn't know what he was talking about, so asked him to explain what he'd just said.

"Oh, didn't Steve tell you what this album is for?" Jonathan asked. I replied by shaking my head "no," so he continued. "That doesn't surprise me. Steve is so quiet about his charity work. I think it's so sacred to him, he just keeps it close to his heart. Anyway, Steve and Katherine started a foundation about fifteen years ago that offers shelter, food, clothing, schooling, medical help, counseling, and job training to those in need. Have you heard of Haven House?"

Yes, I'd heard of Haven House. This was one of the biggest charity organizations in Humanville! It was very famous. I didn't know Steve Barham had anything to do with it and said so to Jonathan.

He answered, "Yeah, I'm sure you didn't. He keeps his involvement pretty quiet. He and Katherine founded it after they had Lily. They recognized there were so many people who had children in less fortunate conditions and wanted to provide a safe haven for them. That's how they came up with the name. Over the years, it has expanded to encompass other areas of need. Those who have been abused, who are homeless, or sick and can't afford medical attention, or who have children and can't care for them properly can get help at Haven House. This was important to Steve and Katherine, partly because of the way Steve and I were raised."

I interjected and said Steve had briefly shared some of his upbringing with me.

Jonathan replied, "I'm glad he did. I don't really enjoy talking about most of it. I've gotten better about being candid for the sake of those who can relate, but it took a long time for me to be able to do that. You see, Steve was my protector when we were kids. I remember times my dad would start to come after me and Steve would step in between us and end up getting the crap beat out of him. It happened so many times. He took so much abuse that was meant for me. I wasn't hit once during my childhood. Steve did everything in his power to prevent it. I was so young when this all started and never knew my mum because she died right after she had me. I had no idea what a parent was, but I knew about love because of Steve. I knew he loved me with all of his heart. When he ran away, he took me with him. He didn't tell you that, did he?"

I said, "No, he didn't. He shared his life on the streets with me and his experience with Mammoth, but I had no idea he was watching over you during all this."

Jonathan answered, "Yeah, it was a dark time. Steve got pretty lost in Humanville, but he never abandoned me. It was kind of amazing, really, for he kept me hidden from all the craziness. I'm still not sure how, but I never saw much of the bad stuff. I bet he didn't tell you about me, did he?"

I replied by saying, "Well, he mentioned he had a younger brother who was born right before his mother died. That's all he said."

Jonathan smiled. "He still protects me, even to this day. I guess it's a habit. He never wanted me to suffer from his celebrity or be in danger because of it. He started making a lot of money shortly after we left my dad's home. I always had clothes and food, and he made sure I went to school every day. I never asked him why he had money or how he got it. All I knew was that he was a better dad to me than my real one had ever been. Once, he went away for a month. Tommy and Claude watched over me until he returned. I thought at the time it was strange he just disappeared, but each time I asked about where he was, the guys told me Steve had gone on a trip and that I was supposed to be on best behavior until he returned. Of course I was, and finally he came back. He gave me no explanation for his absence and I never asked. I didn't find out he'd been arrested until I was out of college. I assume he told you about that. Desmond, I can't imagine what he must have been going through at that point in his life.

"I idolized Steve and always did what he told me to do. That's why I missed a lot of the hell he lived in. I was always studying or playing sports and participating in extra-curricular activities. I ended up being an honor student—got a full scholarship to a pretty prestigious university. Steve was so proud of me for that accomplishment. I was actually in college when he had that horrible accident which almost killed him. I'll never forget how scared I was hearing about it. One of the guys, Tommy actually, called me at school to tell me the news. I flipped out and immediately flew to where he was. I stayed for a couple of weeks, by his side, only leaving to go to get him something he needed or to get a bite to eat. Steve was in a bad way and was delirious for the first week. I thought he was going to die. I didn't know what I was going to do if he didn't make it. I privately made the decision to kill myself if he didn't survive because I wouldn't have been able to bear life without him.

"The second week after the accident, he started to recognize me. He was in a great deal of pain, though, and went through horrible drug withdrawal. It was unbearable to watch. I stayed that week and would've just dropped out of school to be with him, but the guys talked me into going back. Once we all knew he was going to make it, they said he would be terribly disappointed if I blew the semester because of him. I had to agree and begrudgingly returned to campus. I called every day, and over the next couple of months I noticed that Steve not only was recovering but was actually in quite amazing spirits. He would tell me about this eccentric nurse, named Judith, who kept him company and entertained him with her stories. Even though I'd never met her, I felt Steve was in good hands with Judith around."

I interrupted at this point. It was probably rude, but got excited because I knew the story from there.

"Yes! I know about all of this! Steve told me about how he met Katherine." I exclaimed.

Jonathan smiled again, "That's a great story, isn't it? Yes, I was there to witness their meeting. It was a beautiful experience to watch. Well, since you're ahead of me, I'll jump to the present. Steve decided to make this album and donate all the proceeds from record sales to Haven House. The truth is, he basically supports it anyway. He thought the album would be more sacred if it was specifically created for the charity. He has wanted to do this for a very long time but was just so booked up with other commitments. He does recognize, though, that he was supposed to wait until now to complete it. Maybe that's because you were supposed to be involved."

I smiled at that thought and said, "Who knows, it's possible. I'm learning not to second guess God, but to just be open and let love lead the way!"

Jonathan gave me a wink and a "thumbs up" sign at this comment, and we laughed.

He then said, "I oversee all the operational aspects of Haven House. I've been doing it since its inception. I love what I do and get to see miracles every day. You should come down to the headquarters sometime and let me show you around." I told him I'd love to. He suggested maybe later in the week and I said, "sure."

After lunch, he took me back to my car and thanked me for going with him. He then asked for my phone number. (Three guesses on whether I gave it to him or not...you only need one!) He took it and said he'd call me in a couple of days. He smiled and quickly kissed my cheek before driving off. I waved as he left and thought about what a great guy he was. I wondered if he'd really call, but intuitively knew he would. I had a little crush and briefly entertained the idea of kissing him. I wondered whether I should ask God if this was a valid thought but decided not to because I wanted to enjoy my infatuation a little longer. I figured if, for some reason, I was told "no" to these romantic feelings, at least I could have them for a short time. I drove home feeling like a teenager...

HAVEN HOUSE

Sure enough, Jonathan called two days later and I ended up visiting him at Haven House the next afternoon. He walked me through the grounds and buildings, and I was very impressed. He told me there were twenty-three other locations throughout the city, and during the next two hours I saw what Haven House was really all about. As we toured the facility, he explained the goal was to create a renewed sense of self-worth to those who came for help. Each location provided school facilities and job training classes for adults, nurseries, a recreation area, playgrounds, two cafeterias, dormitories, and a couple of little stores where residents could buy clothing, toiletries, books, music, etc. Buses were available to transport children to and from their respective schools. Also, medical and psychological services were available to those who were in need of special attention in these areas.

Jonathan told me that when someone came to Haven House for help, they signed an agreement that stated they would stay for a specific time period. The length of the agreement would vary, depending on how long it would take to educate and train someone for a new, fulfilling direction. Since this place was considered the last hope for most, Jonathan said very few people left early after they had committed to stay, even though they were free to leave at any time. The agreement was mainly a way for someone to feel responsible for his or her word. It was a symbolic gesture, but if someone broke it and left, they could not come back to Haven House at a later time. Now, if they completed their agreement, then for some reason (which was beyond their control) faltered and needed help again, they were welcome to return to Haven House. Jonathan excitedly stated that no one had ever come back. He attributed this to the fact that after someone left, he or she had the confidence to make the love-based decisions that prevented any faltering. I could tell he was very happy about this accomplishment. I saw how much he cared for the people who had been helped here. He seemed like a proud father. I was impressed with his level of passion and commitment.

He continued to say that Steve and Katherine felt it was important to establish a feeling of independence by setting up work responsibilities for every person who resided in the facility. When someone first joined the community, he or she would immediately be assigned a daily task and was paid for this work by "house money." It was a form of currency that was only good in Haven House. Everyone was paid the same hourly wage and most tasks took about the same amount of time. One was not considered better or more prestigious than the next. Haven House emphasized the fact that each individual task contributing to a positive environment was important and that working together for the good of all was worthy of respect and deserved to be compensated. Earning one's room, board, schooling, and training instilled a sense of self-worth, whereas a handout only confirmed a sense of helplessness.

As we kept walking, Jonathan added that Haven House was a place where people learned how to love themselves through a sense of accomplishment, support, love, and trust. Everything was set up on an honor system. There were no clerks in the stores, only a paper to record one's purchases and a box to leave money for items bought. There again, Steve and Katherine believed every person at Haven House needed to understand that they were responsible for every decision they made. If one chose to lie or steal, they had to face the consequences of their fear-based actions.

Jonathan stopped walking for a moment to emphasize this aspect of Haven House. As surprising as it sounds, the energy here was so uplifting and positive, everyone who resided in the facility (whether they were residents or staff) became a family, so there were few secrets. It was relatively easy to discover a troubled soul. If something turned up missing or if money was stolen, the person responsible became known fairly quickly. When the offender was discovered, Jonathan himself would go and have a heart-to-heart talk with him or her. Basically, he'd lovingly say he knew the truth and would then ask what was troubling the person. This would open a discussion that usually ended in an understanding between the two that Haven House was available to help create a new start. One offense would be forgiven, but if the action happened again, Jonathan would know about it again. At that point, the person would be asked to leave and never be allowed to return. In essence, his or her last opportunity here would be gone forever. The consequence for the action would be a return to the streets of Humanville. Throughout the years, only four people had even tried to steal and of those, only one did it again. As promised, he was asked to leave and told he couldn't return. Sure enough, he tried to come back a few months later and had to be turned away. As it turns out, the next year this man had ended up dying under a park bench homeless, destitute, and alcoholic. It broke Jonathan's heart to hear this news, but he had to recognize that the man had chosen his path and that his choice led him to the end result. Decisions made in fear will always ultimately lead to pain and suffering.

Jonathan paused after telling this story. It was apparent the experience had been a difficult one for him. He'd made the only decision he could've made, for integrity is a part of honesty, which is a part of love, which a part of God. Words and actions are the windows to the soul. When the two don't correlate, the person's integrity is questioned and mistrust is created. Respect is lost because the windows are shut and the soul can't shine through. If Jonathan had gone back on his word, the whole foundation of Haven House would've been shaken and mistrust would've developed between everyone involved within the community. Also, the reputation of Haven House would've been damaged, as well as the respect it had achieved. He had no choice, for this man made his own decision and had to be responsible for it. Sometimes, unconditional love can appear on the surface to be cruel, but in reality the opposite is true. Jonathan had to love that man enough to let him be responsible for his choices and actions. He said it was one of the most difficult things he'd ever had to do. I concurred that I would've had the same feelings of heartbreak but added that God was in the man's heart and ultimately was there with him, even in the most painful of times. Jonathan agreed by saying God had told him the same thing, but it had taken much faith to get beyond the experience.

We continued the tour and Jonathan picked up where he had left off by explaining how Haven House operated on a daily basis. He said tasks were assigned depending on one's gifts and talents. For instance, he told me about a young mother with no job skills whose gift was a natural ability to calm a crying baby. She got much joy from caring for infants so was given the task of working in the nursery five hours a day. The remainder of her time was spent in school because she hadn't completed her high school education. She ultimately left Haven House and was able to find work in a childcare facility while she went to college and earned a degree in early child development. This was perfect for her because her children were able to attend the same facility she worked in. Eventually, she became an administrator there and was instrumental in implementing on-premise childcare in many corporate offices.

Another example was about a middle-aged man who'd lost his upper management job and couldn't find other work. He and his family came to Haven House broken-spirited. It was discovered he had a passion for woodworking and carpentry. It had been a hobby, but he loved it. He was assigned to work on the building crew five hours a day. Something always needed to be built or repaired. He found a sense of self-respect every time he built a cabinet or repaired a broken chair. He not only accomplished a goal, but also contributed to the community by utilizing his talents and gifts. The rest of his day was spent in small business job training. His wife attended with him while his two children went to their own school. The man and his family left Haven House after six months. He went to work for an independent carpentry company and after two years became very sought after for his talent and extremely close to the owners. He struck a deal with them and they became partners in a new business. His wife worked right beside him and they ended up flourishing in the industry. They were just one of many families who'd found renewed hope and a new life through Haven House.

As we wrapped up our tour, Jonathan ended by saying the goal at Haven House was not to weigh one's self-worth on monetary means or career achievement. It was to discover one's true gifts and talents and then provide an opportunity to utilize these gifts for the betterment of all. It was obvious that those who entered Haven House came from the streets of Humanville but left residing in Godtown.

When we finished, we went back into Jonathan's office. He asked if I'd like a drink and I said sure, so he went to "fetch" us something. (He had that same adorable accent that Steve had…yes, yes, I had a crush…) While I was waiting for him to return, a thought crossed my mind. I'd been very negative about Haven House when I'd lived in Humanville. I was skeptical of any organization like it. I'd even made fun and had said they were fronts for illegal activities. It was awful. I just didn't believe that an organization could be so pure and love-based. I thought underlying motives were associated with places like this. My attitude about Haven House was typical of my attitude about everything. I perceived life and the world around me through guarded, non-trusting eyes. I didn't understand that Haven House was not a part of Humanville at all but existed in Godtown. I couldn't feel or see Godtown, so I couldn't feel or see love and didn't believe it could be real. I did this with so many things, actually.

Religion was another area of distrust for me. I didn't buy into the beauty of God in organized religion because my perception was jaded by fear and I didn't see God, period. I judged all religion very harshly because I thought religion was judging me. I now finally saw how God exists in all areas of life and can reach each person in a way that he or she will hear. I had been the wrong one, not the other way around. I didn't find God through attending the activities of organized religion, but that was because my heart was so closed and buried in fear. Millions of people have been blessed with the love organized religion can provide in their lives. I will say that human interpretation exists in organized religion and can be as fear-based as any other area of life in Humanville. However, it gives an individual a place to congregate with others who live through love. It also provides the opportunity to learn about the existence of God in our lives, and ultimately can help guide us to our inner voice…our higher self…to where God is inside our hearts and spirits. I can pray for its purity and also rejoice and benefit from the opportunity it provides for loving interaction with other Godtown citizens.

I became very excited about this revelation and started to have a talk with God about it when Jonathan returned with our drinks. I took mine and thanked him. I then asked if there'd be any chance for me to do volunteer work with Haven House. (I know what you're thinking… I had a crush and based on past experience, I bet you think I was motivated by wanting to be near Jonathan instead of desiring to help...nope! I know, it's surprising to me, too, but I really wanted to be of service to this organization. I was sold when we walked by the playground and saw all these beautiful children playing in this secure environment. They looked happy and I wanted to help them continue to live in Godtown, instead of having to go back into Humanville.) Jonathan smiled and said there was definitely an opportunity for me to be involved with Haven House. He'd have the director of volunteers call me the next day. I was happy—really happy—about the possibility of being involved. It felt right.

I finally looked at my watch and saw it was almost five o'clock. I had to run because traffic would be awful and it'd take a while for me to get back home. Jonathan told me it had been a joy to show me around his "world." (Steve had used the same expression the first day I met him at the studio...there's an example of having the same gene pool!) Before he said good-bye, he expressed the hope that we'd see each other again soon. I assured him we would. He offered to walk me to my car, and as I was saying I'd like that, his phone rang and he got into a conversation that sounded like it was going to take awhile. I motioned to him to go ahead and talk, then winked and waved bye as I quietly slid out of his office door. As I was walking down the corridor toward the parking lot, I looked around me and was hit with this wave of peace and fulfillment. I thought it was strange because I'd only felt that on occasion when I was in a studio or singing onstage, and then that one time at the Barhams house. Don't ask me why, but I didn't want to leave. I sauntered down the hall, taking my time, and finally reached the door. I went out into the playground area and saw the same children I'd seen before... playing, laughing, swinging, and running. I just stood there watching, wanting to be out there with them. I knew, at that moment, I'd found the path I needed to go down. I was supposed to be here. This was my new home...

MY NEW HOME...

I started to work at Haven House three days a week and found myself staying longer than my volunteer obligations required because I felt so needed there. I mean, I'd do anything from washing dishes to changing diapers and loved every minute of it. Officially, I was a part of what was referred to as "the talk team." (Boy, was that the hand fitting the glove, or what!?!...absolutely perfect for me!) My job was to interact with the residents and lead a daily, forty-five-minute group gathering that mainly was a show of support and love. The residents were divided into groups of fifteen, and I'd take one of the groups and be in charge of starting an interaction. I'd open the conversation and then encourage the others to share their thoughts. Usually the discussions were passionate, uplifting, and encouraging. Sometimes sensitive subjects would arise, but these talks were just as positive because the residents grew to know that any discussion based on honesty and integrity was a loving interaction. Even if it became un-comfortable, eventually the issue would be resolved through understanding and communication. This was extremely important because the residents learned how to deal with others in a fair, honest, objective way. I got as much out of the gatherings as they did.

At one point, I wondered if I was being selfish by wanting to spend so much time at Haven House because it was so fulfilling. I asked my voice about it. God answered by saying that self-fulfillment through service was very different than being selfish. Selfishness was the act of fulfilling one's own desires at the expense and lack of concern for others. Self-fulfillment was achieving one's aspirations and dreams through one's efforts. When motivated by love and by God, self-fulfillment became selflessness, which was defined as devoting one's self to other's welfare in an unselfish manner. So, in essence, God told me I was fulfilling my own desires as a result of reaching out through love and being of service to those who needed me. Self-fulfillment was a by-product of this loving outreach.

This explanation made total sense to me. I did understand how God had merged with me and why I desired to act in a certain way. When I'd lived in Humanville, fear had driven my actions and they were, for the most part, very self-absorbed and selfish. Now that I resided in Godtown, love was my motivator.

Over the next two months, my volunteer work became the focus of my life. I was still modeling on the occasional job and took singing gigs when I was called for them, but for the most part, I was working at Haven House. If you're wondering how I was surviving, well, I'd get up each morning and say "hello" to my inner voice and ask God to lead me to the places and people I needed to interact with that day. I'd also pray for those I loved and for my needs to be fulfilled. I learned to be very specific in my prayers. Wouldn't you know it, shortly after I started volunteering at Haven House, out of the blue I received a royalty check for the work I did on the Focus Cain album. This surprised me because I thought it wasn't going to be out for some time. Apparently, their label decided to release the first single early and it was getting quite a bit of airplay. I sang on it, so there you go. I hadn't been listening to the radio for some time (I'd take a break every so often when I felt overwhelmed with the whole music thing), so I had no idea it was being played. Cool, huh!?! As a result, financial strain was alleviated for awhile. I'm still amazed how love will fulfill my every need when I get out of my own way and let it provide for me.

I increased my work time at Haven House from three to four days a week after the third month. One day, Jonathan came by and asked me come to his office. Oh, for the most part, I rarely saw Jonathan while I was working. The volunteer program rotated its workers to all of the Haven House locations, so I'd be at one for a week, then transfer to another one the next week, etc. I hadn't been assigned to the headquarters until the week Jonathan requested to talk to me. I thought you might be interested in knowing this information just in case you were still questioning my motives for being involved. (Aww... you trust me by now!)

I followed him to his office. He asked me to sit down, then did the same behind his desk. He just stared at me with that half smile, half-pondering look. I was confused. He didn't say anything, so I finally said in exasperation, "What!?!" He laughed out loud and answered, "All right, all right. Sorry, I was trying to formulate my thoughts, here. Desmond, I have something to ask you. Please don't answer immediately. I want you to think it over before you say anything. You see, I haven't told you this, but I've been trying to get the board of directors to open up a new position at Haven House for about a year because I'm just too overwhelmed to address all of the needs here. I also wanted to be sure that if I encouraged them to allocate funds for a new position, I'd be able to fill it with the right person. I've found the person, if she's available and interested in accepting the job."

I gotta tell you, I consider myself pretty bright. However, on occasion I do completely blow that perception and let something completely go over my head. This was one of those times. I had no idea who he was thinking about hiring. I was totally focusing on what he was saying and shaking my head every so often in the "uh-huh, uh-huh" motion. When he was finished, my response was, "Hmm. What's the position?"

Jonathan said, "Officially, it's called Director of Public Outreach. What this really means is that this person will be in charge of publicity, charity events, public relations outside the organization, and special programs dealing with Haven House. It's a pretty broad job description, but in essence, it's an extremely creative position. In fact, the album you sang on will be handled through this office. It also involves public speaking. The person in this position will be the voice for Haven House."

I said, "Wow, Jonathan, this sounds like such a great job. Who do you have in mind for it?"

He just sat there with a surprised look on his face, then smiled. "Desmond, I'm offering this job to *you* if you want it. I think it'd be perfect for you because it would utilize all of your gifts and talents. I'd even want you to give concerts and bring in other performers to sing with you during some of the events we'll do for public awareness."

I was blown away! Me? For some reason, it never entered my mind I could be in the running for a job like this. I sat back in my chair and didn't respond. I just thought for a minute...this was perfect for me. I could use my voice, performing talent, education, creative spirit, social skills, and best of all, I'd be working for Haven House. I finally looked back at Jonathan and said, "Really?" (I obviously hadn't taken my extended vocabulary class yet!)

Jonathan replied, "Yes, really."

I said, "I don't know what to say. Can I think about it for a couple of days and let you know?"

He said, "I'd hope you'd put a great deal of thought and prayer into your decision, so please take as much time as you need, as long as you let me know while we are still young enough to walk without canes!"

I think he was kidding about the cane part, but I told him I'd respond before the end of the week. He said that would great, then had to run to a meeting, so said he'd call me later in the evening. I walked out of his office in a trance.

What a surprise...me, working, really working, at Haven House. I was taken aback because this was so unexpected. I kind of floated down the hall in deep thought. I had been praying every day for God to guide me to where I was needed to fulfill my purpose. I'd been told to continue to let love guide me and to have no fear. I tried to trust that my path would be shown to me and look what had just happened. The power of love is so awe-inspiring. I immediately checked in with my inner voice. I had to confirm that this was what I thought it was...

Me: I can't believe what just happened in Jonathan's office. Did you do this?

God: You know the answer to that question. We did this, together. You prayed to be of service to the universe and to be shown your path to fulfilling your purpose. You sincerely got out of your own way and did not let fear enter into your decisions. You have allowed Me to guide you and have realized you found happiness while you were going through the process of following your path. You now understand the beauty of the process. Your motivations have been your desire to love those around you and to be the light of love in their lives. You let go of an agenda and let love flow through you. You have finally stepped out of your "box" and are thinking in a broader sense. You can now also see how prayer works. You and I have created this blessing, together. Rejoice in the new opportunity to experience love.

Me: God, You're amazing. I know this new career opportunity is a gift and thank you for Your love and belief in me.

God: You are welcome. Now you must thank yourself, for you were just as instrumental in the creation of this blessing as I was. We are one. You have merged with Me, and I shine through you.

Me: I do know this and am excited about life and the future. I have so much hope for the world and for Humanville. I want to be an example of love in motion. I do believe everyone has the ability to live in Godtown. I desire to help make this happiness a reality in other lives.

God: Yes, you do. Now, make your decision and commit to it.

Me: You know what I'm going to do, don't you?

God: We are one, correct?

Me: Yes, we are. God...I have to ask...will I be good at this work?

God: Anything you do through love will be very successful. This is My promise to you. Know you are blessed and remember fear has no power in your life as long as you let love lead your way.

Me: As always, You're so right. I love you!...I know, I know, don't say it.
I love myself, too. I'm going to go tell Jonathan the decision. Wanna
come?

God: I'm already there...

With that, I turned around and ran back to Jonathan's office. I burst through
the door, then remembered he had a meeting, so he wasn't even there. I
went over to his desk, found a clean sheet of paper, wrote "yes" in huge
letters on it, then taped it to his chair. I signed it "D" and hoped this was
official enough for him. I laughed as I left, thinking, "Oh boy, I'm acting
like I'm accepting a marriage proposal here!" It suddenly dawned on me
that it was one, in a way. I was committing to something I believed in,
loved, and honored. Hmm, very similar...I didn't know if Haven House was
truly ready for my unique ways of doing things, but I figured it would all
turn out ok. I mean, convention had never worked for me, but who said
taking a "real" job had to be conventional? I was about to rock and roll.
This would be the best gig of my life....

TODAY...

Ok, bet you thought you'd never get here, did you? The truth is, neither did I. It's still hard to believe at times! Years have passed since the infamous "girls night out" (which started this whole thing), but it seems like yesterday. Like I mentioned, time has flown! There are still a few details I need to tell you before ending my story.

I assume you're curious to find out if Jonathan and I ended up together, right? Well, we did become very close. When I started volunteering at Haven House, we spent a lot of free time with each other going rollerblading, jogging, shopping, bicycling etc. We'd hang out at each other's homes, cook meals together, or grab a bite to eat after work. I told him about my struggles with anorexia and bulimia and also about my family and friends, how I'd found my inner voice, etc. He shared his experience of discovering his inner voice. He also told me some things I'd not known about his life. Unbeknownst to me, he'd been engaged a few years before we met, but had lost his fiancé in a car accident. It'd been a devastating experience for him. His faith in love and God gave him insight to survive the loss and he eventually appreciated the fact that she'd fulfilled her purpose here and was in the next phase of her life and journey. He said he still missed her, though, and I could tell she lived on in his heart. He also told me about how he and Steve had healed their relationship with their father and had been able to share quite a few wonderful years with him before he passed away. He was residing in Godtown at the time of his death and Jonathan was full of thanks for that blessing.

As we got closer, we both recognized the fact that we'd been brought together by love, but the love we shared wasn't romantic. In some ways, it was just as unconditional and beautiful, and we've continued to cherish our friendship over the last seven years. Not only is Jonathan one of my best friends, he is a part of my family. We still talk almost every day and spend as much time together as possible.

As for my work...I found incredible fulfillment at Haven House. As you know, I accepted the position Jonathan offered me and started without a clue as to what I was doing. I winged it for some time and of course didn't stay within convention at all. I did everything in what I like to refer to as a "special" way. I think the board of directors had other terminology for my methods! They grew to appreciate me over time, though. We ended up getting a ton of media attention because Haven House set precedent in the area of public awareness through of some of my wacky events. For instance, I decided to have a parade to announce the release of the album Steve produced for the organization. I somehow finagled permission from the Humanville city council for this event (which was, itself, a miracle). I mean, we went all out...clowns, floats, bands, horses, fireworks, and even elephants. I will say the elephants were a bit much, for one of them decided to sit down right in the middle of the parade, and we couldn't get her up for thirty minutes. She just wanted to rest, I guess. Didn't think elephants rested that way really, but this one did. Anyway, overall it was quite the show and the community actually dug it. (Humanville can be so stuffy and caught up with appearances, I wondered how it would react to this. The people who came had a great time, despite themselves!) I loved every minute of bringing joy into the streets of Humanville.

Another great memory was the time I put on a concert for the city in City Park. Since I had Steve's assistance, I was able to get huge stars to perform, including Jacob Richards and Mammoth. It was an amazing night. We had media coverage that spread throughout the world because of the caliber of performers, and we raised millions from the live recording album and the media deals we negotiated for broadcast coverage. I got to sing back-up with Jacob and at the end of the night, all the artists joined me onstage to sing the final song. Ok, so it was a little corny, I didn't care... it was an incredible experience and we even received a standing ovation! I spoke to the audience before we said goodnight and thanked them for supporting Haven House and their fellow humans. Since it was a free concert, there were literally 500,000 people who attended. Sounds impossible, doesn't it? Well, when major stars offer to sing for free, people show up!

Oh, I need to tell you that I even invited Trinity Lyons to be a part of it. She had ended up releasing two albums, but never really hit because her music was not sincere and the public rejected it. She went through what she referred to as a "necessary humiliation" and tried every manipulation she could think of to resurrect her failing career. Her fear was in control, though, and it just didn't happen for her. Through this experience, she was humbled enough to be blessed with hearing the "whisper" of God. She opened her heart over the next year and eventually became a citizen of Godtown, also. We actually became friends after we bumped into each other at an ice hockey game, and she now is a part of a band that has done quite well in the last couple of years. They perform a very cool style of music that focuses on positive lyrics while being extremely groove-driven. It attracts a young fan base that is definitely in need of their music. I'm happy for her. She also told me that she and Lou ended their relationship after her second album failed, and she never heard from him again. However, she read in an industry magazine that the next year he was caught embezzling money from his other clients. He was convicted and sentenced to five years in jail, where apparently he still is today...hmmmm.

As it turned out, Steve's album sold over five million copies. I had no idea whether people would appreciate the nature of the music, but I should've realized that the power of love permeated through every note of this record, and it touched people's hearts. Even those who were in the depths of Humanville seemed to react to it. They probably didn't understand what they were feeling but gravitated to the music anyway. The money generated by record sales went to building a new medical facility that treated individuals who couldn't afford other health care or who were extremely ill and had been dropped by their health coverage. (Humanville's health care system was horrible and private coverage was even worse. Sick or injured individuals were at the mercy of corporate or political decision-makers who only thought in terms of "how much is this one going to cost?") Haven House was a facility that embraced the sick and injured and gave them an opportunity to have quality health care when Humanville turned them away, which was quite often.

Steve continued to produce hit records, and he and Katherine watched Lily and Rose grow into beautiful young women. Lily graduated from undergraduate studies with a 3.95 G.P.A. and went on to medical school, where she is currently excelling in her studies. She wants to become a surgeon. She's not sure about a specialty area but has found a passion in helping the elderly. I can't wait to see where she lands.

Rose is following in her father's footsteps. She is a terrific singer and Steve finally let her get in the studio and try out her chops. He had hesitated to rush her because he didn't want her to get ahead of herself and not be ready to handle the unstable side of the industry. I have to say Rose is one of the most balanced young women I've ever encountered. I think she'll be fine in the "crazy" music environment. She's mature and her motivations are love-based. She recognizes her gift and knows she needs to share it.

Julie ended up marrying the professor I told you about. She is blissfully happy and has two children. She now sings only for pleasure and actually helps me as often as possible when I plan big events. She's a great organizer and I rely heavily on her talents and skills.

Jonathan met and married a wonderful woman three years ago. They met in the most unlikely of places...the batting cages. I know, that's something, isn't it? Her name is Genevieve and she's from Jonathan's homeland. He would go to the cages every so often to just goof around and unwind, and one day there she was, actually hitting a 70 mph fastball! She had played sports when she was younger and was very athletic. She went to the batting cages to just have fun. She was adorable and petite but full of fire and passion. He went over to the cage next to where she was batting and started hitting but couldn't keep his concentration. He was terrible! She couldn't help but laugh a couple of times at his sloppy attempts to impress her, and he finally broke the ice and started talking to her. They ended up meeting at a close-by restaurant for coffee where they told each other a little bit about themselves.

She was nurse practitioner at the time, and get this, for it's...well, it's God, actually. Genevieve's family lived on the next block over from where Jonathan's dad lived, and Steve actually went to school with her older brother. Isn't that amazing? They became inseparable immediately, and married six months after they met. They are so happy and I adore her. Since their marriage, Genevieve has left her nursing practice and now works at Haven House, also. When she was growing up in Humanville, a distant relative—who visited the family quite often—sexually abused her. This nightmare left deep, emotional scars. Her anger and fear manifested into extremely wild behavior and she spent her teenage years and early twenties in the throws of alcohol, drugs, and other forms of self-abuse. She discovered her inner voice at twenty-four and turned her life around by listening to God's direction and finding a love for herself through God. She became a citizen of Godtown and desired to devote her life to helping others who have gone through the same experience she did. When she came to work for Haven House, she created a program that specifically focuses on healing the wounds that are caused by sexual abuse. It has been extremely successful, and she does a great deal of public speaking on the subject. She emphasizes that the opportunity for healing comes from the power of love and God and that there is no need for shame. I admire her honesty and courage, and I'm thrilled Jonathan is blessed with such an incredible wife. They have one little boy, who looks just like his father but has his mother's passion and fire.

As for me, I did meet someone a few years after starting to work at Haven House. He's an attorney, and Haven House is one of his biggest clients. We met at the City Park concert I put together. He'd done all the legal work for the event—which was a huge undertaking—and I'd talked to him on the phone many times but didn't meet him face to face until that night. I was running around like a mad woman and he was backstage, just observing and being way too calm. I noticed him early on, and even in my frenzy, still managed to pass by him, oh, I'd say about twenty-four times. I went from avoiding eye contact with him to smiling as I passed by, then to saying "hi", and finally, stopping for a second to ask him some silly question I'd come up with just to talk to him. At the end of the night, he walked over to where I was standing and officially introduced himself. He said his name was Gregory Roberts. He extended his hand in greeting, and when I touched him I felt a wave of energy hit me like a bolt of lightening. I just froze. I mean, here I was in the middle of extreme chaos, and the world suddenly stopped. I looked into his eyes and knew I'd found my life mate. It was one of the wildest experiences I've ever had. He asked if I'd like to join him for a late dinner after the event was over, and I said yes, which was insane because I had all these people around me who assumed I was going to hang with them. I couldn't help myself. Jonathan, being the friend he is, witnessed this and came over to me and said he'd take care of everyone. He told me to not worry and to go enjoy myself. He knew Gregory extremely well, for they had worked together a very long time, and he was aware that Gregory lived in Godtown, also. Before he walked away, he leaned down and whispered, "Desmond, congratulations." He felt it, too. It figures, we're so connected. I looked at him and then hugged him so hard he actually lost his breath for a second. I didn't mean to do that but was just excited!

I did go out with Gregory that night, then the next, and then the next. I discovered he was kind, intelligent, passionate, compassionate, witty, honest and had integrity. Most of all, he knew how to love without fear and allowed me to love him without fear. We both trusted God's guidance and grew to love each other in a way I didn't know was possible. Things moved fairly quickly, and we married a year after we met. The wedding was small and intimate, but our families were there, and of course our dearest friends.

Speaking of my family, today we are all extremely close and I can only tell you that love is a miracle-maker. My mother and father came to visit me shortly after I started working at Haven House and were overwhelmed with the changes they saw in me. We stayed up all night on the fourth day they were here and talked until the morning light. I told them everything about my anorexia and bulimia, about overhearing the people in the coffee shop, and about the old woman in the park. I didn't know how they'd respond, but

God had assured me things would go wonderfully, and sure enough, they did. I fell deeply in love with my parents, and I think they finally understood me. We cried and laughed, and they told me how sorry they were for not recognizing the struggle I'd gone through and for not being more understanding during my battles. I told them they'd done the best they could have done, considering I didn't let them into my heart. I assured them I was healed through love and through God, and then I told them about Godtown. They were very supportive of my experience. I apologized for closing them off from my heart and soul for so long. It was a pretty amazing visit, and it changed my relationship with them forever. Today they, too, are citizens of Godtown and are my best friends, along with my husband and Jonathan. I cherish every moment I spend with them. I've also bonded with my siblings and their families. We try to get together as much as possible, for we have a lot of fun together.

I'm happy, I'm in love, I give and receive love, I get to use my gifts to help others, and I'm beautifully rewarded for this service. I am singing, laughing, playing, working, and living through love. I live with God as my guide and inspiration. God lives in me and shines through me. I've not dealt with bulimia or anorexia for seven years, and although I think about my past struggles from time to time, I have no fear of the diseases ever returning to my life. Love has replaced the fear. I choose to listen to my voice....my higher self...to God every day, and love never fails me. I have learned to trust the power of God and know I'm in the arms of love at all times.

Ok, I've got to let you in on a little secret. I haven't even told Gregory yet, but I'm also pregnant. Can you believe it? I just officially found out today, but I already knew. Yes, God told me, and I could tell. I'm so excited, I'm about to jump out of my skin!!! I'll tell Gregory and my family tonight. This is such a miracle! To think I was so afraid of this for so many years...

So, you see, that's why I haven't written sooner. I know you understand, but I wanted to explain, anyway. Now, there's one more thing I need to tell you. Remember my *Godtown Guideline Handbook*? Well, I've been waiting for God to direct me to the person I'm supposed to pass it along to. I've waited many years and finally have been told it's time. I knew I'd give it to someone very special, and of course, you are. I was hoping to pass it along in person, but "my condition" kind of stopped that plan, so God and I thought this letter would be the next best thing. I can't tell you how thrilled I am that you're the one! I never ceased to be amazed at the power of love.

With that, I'll close. Please know I'll be thinking about you and praying for your happiness and joy. My hope is that our paths will cross in the very near future. You never know, anything's possible when we listen...

Love,
Desmond

THE
GODTOWN GUIDELINE
HANDBOOK

listen

ABOUT THE AUTHOR

Cynthia French grew up in the corporate world. Her father worked for a major oil company, so she spent her childhood moving back and forth from Oklahoma to Texas. After graduating from college, Cynthia moved to Los Angeles, CA with the intention of finishing her graduate studies in Arts Administration (which she started at Oklahoma State University, after completing her Bachelor of Science Degree.) She joined a small church there (which had a strong entertainment industry congregation), and started singing solos. Before long, she found herself getting hired for studio work and gigs. This opened the door to a professional career as a vocalist and musician. She toured in Europe, Australia, and the Orient during her time in Los Angeles.

While still living on the west coast, she traveled to Nashville, TN to explore the country music scene and fell into a unique opportunity to sing on the Grand Ole Opry during her first visit. This prompted her to move to Nashville to pursue an artist/songwriter career. Within a matter of months, Cynthia had secured publishing, management, and production deals. Shortly after completing her contractual writer/artist duties with these companies, she founded an independent music publishing company, which has been in operation since 1995.

Cynthia has also provided background vocals on a number of records, including Reba McIntyre's "If You See Him" album, which produced the number one song "Forever Love." She has also worked on many alternative rock and pop albums, and is in the process of recording a new CD of her own original music.

Currently dividing her time between Nashville and Los Angeles, Cynthia continues to work in the music industry. Recently, she has begun touring the country speaking publicly about her experiences with eating disorders, how she overcame them, and what led her to create this novel.

ACKNOWLEDGMENTS

I express my great appreciation to the following people:

My Family:
Gilbert French, Carolyn French, Ron Garrison, Susan Garrison, Brian French, Lori French, Andrea Garrison, Josh Garrison, Lindsey Garrison, Evan French, and Garrett French. I am so very grateful to all of you for the wonderful and strong foundation you have given me. I am proud to be a part of this family and love you all very much.

My Relatives:
To my extended family...aunts, uncles, and cousins. I am so amazed at how much we have grown, both in numbers and in love. You have consistently believed in me, and shown excitement each time I've brought a new story or adventure home to share. Thank you for your patient ears and support!

The sisterhood:
Cassandra Berns, Calina Cook, Alisha Davis, Karen Faye, Beth Hooker, JK Jones, Kathleen Lague, Sharyn Lane, Rebecca McCabe, Michele McCord, Randi Mavestrand, Randi Michaels, Tracy Nei, Kim Parent, Vaughan Penn, Colette O'Connell, Jill Riley, Peggy Seagren, Winnie Thexton, and Marisa Wayne. All of you have shown great love and support, given me the gift of laughter, helped me through tears, and walked side by side with me while we've followed our dreams. You are so very precious and my love for you is everlasting.

The Friends:
Harry Brobst, Robert Shabkie, Andrew Lessman, Dan Kough, Laurie Kerr, Charlie Daniels, Jr., Lora Daniels, George McCabe, Bob Seagren, Ansel Davis, Thorston Heintz, Scott Francis, Hawk Wolinski, Gary Harrison, Bob Doyle, Joe Henry, Tony Horton, Matthew Bennett, Frank Stallone, Skip Ewing, Jason Padgett, Allen Butler, Hillary Butler, Michelle Metzger, Liz Rose, Greg Richardson, Ernie Williams, Steven McClintock, Cathy Ann Whitworth, Gunnar Nelson, Matthew Nelson, Yvette Nelson, Terra Shapiro, Mary Glenn McCombs, Greta Gaines, Stacey Mitchell, Mark McQuinn,

John Foster, Lynn Foster, Gwendelyn Beck, Gary Belz, Lord Lawrence Oliver, Will Ward, Kevin Doughtery, John Briggs, Paul Craft, Dave Goodwin, Jim Kimball, Juan Contrarous, Max Hutchinson, Dean Miller, Bill Kimberlin, Becky Hobbs, Duane Shaqua, Paul McCombs, Carla McCombs, Bobby Blazier, Ron Hemby, Kim Patton, Carolyn Cole J.D. Martin, Lisa Peeples, Andy Goldmark, Sume Goldmark, Patty Rocha, Melody Malloy, David Malloy, Michael Eidel, Gregg Brown, Brett Berns, Sara Berns, Dub Cornett, Peter Durgee, Tara Durgee, Tourkwell Creevy, John Jackson, Eric Estok, Scott LaFeet, Kodua Michelle, Don Norman, Reece Faw, Debbie Zatzison, Tracy Cox, Mandy Lawson, Karen Sherrill, Laura Putty, Melissa Raitt, Adair Johnson, Valerie DeMarco, The Genth Family, Kent Dunlap, Corde Dunlap, Donna Bailey, Debbie Cowart, and Nancy Freeman. All of you have made an impact on my life and have blessed me with your friendship throughout the years. I thank you.

The very private thoughts:

Mom and Dad, you are my lifeblood. What you've done to show your belief in me is almost beyond my ability to comprehend. You are my best friends and I'm so lucky to be a part of you, and am proud to have you as my parents. Thank you for loving me so purely, and for trusting and believing in me. I love you with every breath I take.

Susan, I'm grateful we've become close again. I idolized you when we were children, I respect you now that we're adults and am honored to be your little sister. Your faith is beautiful and your ability to nurture is a true gift. I'm so proud of you and love you very much. To Ron, Andrea, Josh, and Lindsey, I love you, and hope your dreams come true. You are all very special to me.

Brian, you're my baby brother. I could not be more proud of you for your accomplishments and talents. You're an inspiration to me as a parent and as a human being. Thank you for all your patience while you coached me on how to use a computer! You're one of the most extraordinary people I've ever met and I love you very, very much. To Lori, Evan, and Garrett, thank you for being such a beautiful part of this family. You all bless us very much.

Robert, thank you for all the years of unconditional love, and for teaching me how to trust love. You have never turned away from me, and will always be my soul brother. Also, thanks for all the clothes. You've made me a princess in more ways than one. You are, and will always be, my prince.

Harry, what would I have done without your friendship? You have believed in me from the start of my college career, and your words of support have carried me through many a difficult time. I am so thankful for you and think that you've made this planet a much better place to live for ninety-two years. It (or I) wouldn't be the same without you! I'll love you forever.

Andrew, you've carried on the role that Harry began in my life. Your undying belief in my talents, gifts, and abilities have been an inspiration in far more ways than you probably even know. I'm so very proud of you, and feel blessed to have you in my life. I want you to know how much I appreciated your focus and your input on this book. Your constructive suggestions helped create a much stronger story, and it meant the world to me that you cared enough about its message to put such energy into it. Thank you for the many years of love and support.

Cassie, you are a true member of my family. I am so very grateful to have you in my life! My belief in your talents is immeasurable, and my support for your dreams is unshakable. You can reach them! Thank you for all the memories and your love.

Rebecca, what can I say? You have taught me confidence through example. I'm so happy for you, and cherish our sisterhood. I know you will be a phenomenal mother, and will be able to balance your life with grace and finesse.

Beth, you are one of the most talented women I have ever met, and I am honored to have you involved with this book. The artwork is phenomenal, and it reflects its artist. I am proud to have your work on the cover of "Humanville". Your vision made my words come alive. Thank you.

Sharyn, you've spoiled me with your beautiful friendship. You have blessed my life so much. You are special, talented, beautiful, bright, and wise. An inspiration to me!

Alisha, God-bless your marriage. You'll do great! Thank you for all those words of wisdom at very important moments, and for all the fun.

Calina, thank you for being a great travel companion and for the challenging conversations we shared on those lonely roads. Your strength is an example to everyone around you!

Michele, you've been with me since the beginning of this "Nashvegas" experience…memories, tears, laughs, triumphs, and heartaches. We've survived to tell about it. Thank you for including me in your work and dreams.

Vaughan, you helped me find my vocal and songwriting muse, and allowed me to create wonderful music with you. We became family in the process.

Tracy, I'm so happy that you've become such a big part of my life. Thank you for your undying love and support (and never ending smile).

Marisa, I miss seeing your beautiful face! You hold such a special place in my heart. I believe you are one of the most phenomenal women I've ever met, and am so grateful for your friendship.

Karen, you are my sister. You have been a shining example of strength, spirituality, love, and perseverance. Thank you for the years of friendship, and for your continual love and encouragement…and for making me look so great in photos. Your talent is unbelievable!

Randi Mavestrand, you are also my sister, and I admire your talent, and your courage. You looked deep inside yourself, which is so very commendable. You are also an example of strength and perseverance.

Winnie, (yes, another sister!) you are so beautiful! Your youth and vigor never cease to amaze me. I am so grateful for your friendship, and for all the great memories. We have many more to make!

Colette, I give thanks to Tokyo and Hiroshi, for they brought you to me. Your friendship has meant the world, and I cherish it. I hope every one of your dreams and goals come true, and that you have a lifetime of happiness and joy.

Peggy, wow, what a ride, huh? Who thought that sixteen years ago our lives would turn out the way that they have? I thank you for your undying belief in me, and for your continual words of encouragement. I think you are a very gifted woman, and I hope you never let go of your dreams. You deserve to fulfill them!

Dan, you have become an important part of our family, and I adore you! Thank you for your wit, kindness, intelligence, and love. You bless everyone around you.

Hawk, we have had a long and interesting friendship, and I've appreciated your belief in my talents. Thank you. I admire your creative abilities. I'm glad you're finally stateside again. Welcome home!

Matt and Gun, I admire your strength, perseverance, and talent. You have blessed my life, and my hope is that all of your hard work and creative pursuits will continue to bring you success and happiness. Yvette, you are truly beautiful, and a wonderful vocalist. Terra, I'm so glad you've become a part of our lives. Thank you all for your friendship.

Steven, Cathy Ann, and Tessa, I'm glad that we've been able to become closer friends. Steven, thank you for your help in "dot.com" land. I appreciate you're watchful eye on that one!

Gary, you have seen me through many experiences and have been a constant source of strength. You are very talented, kind, and a very good father. I have appreciated our friendship. Thank you.

Matthew, I'm thankful we've come back into each other's lives. I appreciate your support with this book, and for all the laughter you created in Nashville. You really did brighten the place up! May all your desires and dreams come true.

Tony, I am excited for your new path. You are such a special person, and I'm happy our friendship has been renewed. Thank you for your belief in this book and for your willingness to help me place it.

Michelle M., thank you for being such a support system in this crazy music industry. Your belief in my songs and writers gave me continual encouragement. A special friend.

JK, you are such a light and joy to be around. You are one of my angels.

Randi Michaels, I am happy for you in your new life. I thank you for the years of memories.

Jill, you've helped me grow in more ways than I even planned on, really. I am happy for your newfound path.

Liz, you have also taught me a lot about myself. I thank you for the opportunity to get into the publishing business.

Skip, thank you for Hawaii.